SCENT OF FURY

A CHRISTIAN ROMANTIC SUSPENSE

SULLIVAN K9 SEARCH AND RESCUE

LAURA SCOTT

READSCAPE PUBLISHING, LLC

1

A heavy thudding sound woke Trina Warren from sleep. Blinking in the dim light, she frowned, straining to listen. It took her a moment to remember she shared her house with her eight-year-old nephew, Ben. The boy was her responsibility now that her older sister had passed away from a tragic biking accident back in May. With a grimace, Trina jumped out of bed, shoved her feet into a pair of slippers, and opened the door to the hallway.

Ben's previously closed bedroom door hung ajar.

"Ben? Is everything okay?" She pushed his door open, expecting to see him in bed, but the room was empty.

A shiver of panic snaked down her spine. "Ben? Where are you?"

No response. Moving quickly through her small three-bedroom house, it didn't take long for her to verify that the boy was nowhere to be found.

Her stomach knotted as she hurried back to Ben's room. Flipping on the light switch, she scanned the room. As usual, it was a mess, but she grimly realized his shoes and favorite long-sleeved western-style shirt were missing, along with the brand-new school backpack she'd purchased for him last week.

A sense of dread seeped into her bones. Ben had been struggling with the loss of his mother and with the move from Laramie to Cody. Her sister had lived in an apartment after her divorce from Ben's father who had taken off when Ben was five. At the time, Trina had thought bringing Ben to live at her house, giving him a fresh start here in Cody, had been the better option.

Now she wasn't so sure.

Praying he hadn't done anything stupid, she spun around and bolted outside. At five thirty in the morning, dawn was just breaking over the horizon. Raking her gaze over the area, she searched for him. "Ben! Ben, where are you?"

The early morning breeze rustled the leaves on the trees. Dew on the grass dampened her slippers. Her home was in the northwest corner of Cody, close to the local nature trail. Ben had looked at her in disgust when she'd suggested hiking the trail a few days ago. Maybe because of the way his mother had died in a mountain bike accident? She wasn't sure what he'd been thinking. Ben hadn't opened up to her. She wasn't even sure he said much to his psychologist.

Would he have gone for an early morning hike on his own?

It didn't seem likely, but she wasn't sure where else he would have gone. Swallowing hard, she turned and ran back inside. She swapped her slippers for hiking boots and drew on a sweatshirt. Early mornings in August could be chilly. First, she'd go through the neighborhood, then check the trail. Maybe he hadn't gone far.

Trina grabbed her phone, then paused when she noticed one of the kitchen cabinet doors was open. Obviously, Ben had taken more than just his backpack. She turned and headed outside. Considering he'd taken his backpack, she didn't really think he'd be in the neighborhood but forced herself to walk up and down the streets anyway. When she didn't find him, she jogged through her backyard to the shortcut that would take her to the nature trail.

If she didn't find Ben soon, she would call the Sullivans for help. She'd gone to high school with the twins, Joel and Justin Sullivan. At one time, she'd harbored a crush on Joel, but the day she'd hoped to ask him to homecoming, she'd found him with Bethany, one of the high school cheerleaders. They'd made a striking pair with Joel's dark hair and Bethany's long blond tresses. Trina with her straight red hair and freckles looked like Peppermint Patty from the Snoopy cartoon, so she'd kept her distance after that.

The Sullivan family was well known throughout the region for their search and rescue services. Trina walked along the path, concerned because there were points where the trail paralleled the path of the Shoshone River, which flowed rapidly enough to be dangerous.

Especially to a child who hadn't grown up in the area.

"Ben!" She followed the trail to the south, hoping that was the direction he'd taken. But really, he could have gone either way.

After ten minutes of not seeing him, she turned and ran in the opposite direction. How far could an eight-year-old walk anyway? She had no idea.

The incline was steeper along the north path, and after a few minutes, she gave up. Her voice was hoarse from yelling his name. If Ben hadn't stayed on the trail, he could have been anywhere.

She pulled out her phone and called the Sullivan ranch. Even at barely six in the morning, her call was quickly answered by a female voice. "Sullivan K9 Search and Rescue."

"Good morning. My name is Trina Warren, and my eight-year-old nephew, Ben Warren, is missing. I—we live in Cody. I went to school with Joel and Justin and need help, fast."

"Of course. Joel and Royal are free to help." The woman's tone was cheerful yet calm. "What's your address?"

Trina rattled off the information.

"Great. I'll give him your contact information, okay? He'll call when he's on the road."

"Thank you." Knowing help was on the way brought a wave of relief. After pocketing her phone, she decided to keep going up the path. After all, she knew it would take almost forty-five minutes for Joel to get there.

Maybe she'd find Ben before then.

She continued walking, scanning both sides of the path for any sign of Ben. Her earlier annoyance with his going off on his own had morphed into fear. What if he'd tripped, fallen, and hit his head? Her sister, Evie, had died of a severe head injury.

She couldn't bear the thought of losing Ben the same way.

For a moment, she thought of Ben's father. Brian Ashland had made it clear he had no desire to be married or tied down to a child. Evie had gotten pregnant right after high school. Brian had gotten a job in Laramie, so Evie and Ben had moved there too. They'd gotten married, but things had not gone well for the young couple. Trina hadn't been surprised when Brian left. Evie had been glad to be rid of him, having confided that Brian's drinking had gotten worse over the years, and when he was drunk, he slapped her around. In Trina's opinion, Evie was better off without him.

The one who'd suffered the most was Ben. As a five-year-old, he hadn't understood the undercurrents between his parents. One day his father was there, the next Brian was gone.

Her phone rang, startling her. Pulling it from her pocket, she quickly answered. "Hello?"

"Trina? Is that you?"

Joel's husky voice almost brought tears to her eyes. Until that moment, she'd carried the weight of Ben's absence alone. "Yes. Sorry, my voice is hoarse. I've been hiking the trail calling for Ben."

"Understandable," Joel said reassuringly. "I'm on my way, should be there in fifteen minutes or so."

"Thank you." He'd made good time, and she turned to head back home. There was no point in wandering around. She knew Joel's K9, Royal, would be able to find Ben. "I appreciate your help."

"I'll need dirty socks or T-shirts from your nephew to use as a scent source for Royal," Joel said.

"Trust me, his room has plenty of dirty clothes strewn about." She tried to smile, but fresh tears pricked her eyes instead. "I'm heading home now."

"Sounds good. Don't worry, my black lab Royal is a great tracker."

"I'm glad." She swiped at her face. "See you soon."

"Soon," he echoed, before ending the call. Shoving her phone back into her pocket, she picked up the pace. She was convinced Joel and his K9 would find Ben. Especially if the boy had left the trail.

Ben would be okay. Tired, hungry, and maybe sore if he'd fallen, but he'd be fine.

She couldn't bear the thought of finding the young boy seriously hurt or worse.

JOEL USED his thumb to end the call with Trina. He remembered her from high school, although they hadn't shared many classes. She'd been a quiet, shy girl who'd preferred books over people.

He hadn't known her nephew was staying with her and wondered if that was a temporary summer vacation kind of thing or something more permanent. Not that it mattered. A missing child was always a high priority.

His phone rang again, but this time Lisa's name popped up on the screen. With a low groan, he quickly hit the end call button, sending her to voice mail. This was the third time she'd called this week. It had been a mistake to give Lisa Schilling his number. The strikingly beautiful female hiker he and Royal had found and rescued over a month ago now had mistaken his concern for her welfare as something more. She'd repeatedly asked him to lunch and dinner. He'd tried to let her down gently, but she had continued calling anyway. He'd been even more concerned when she'd let him know she'd moved to Wyoming from Arizona. Again, he'd told her he was busy with SAR work, but she claimed she loved it here.

He'd suspected she'd moved for him.

Justin told him to block her number. And after this week, he was on board with that plan. Why was she calling him so early in the morning anyway? Was there a problem of some sort? He resisted the urge to call her back. More likely she was being persistent, accustomed to getting her way. Bethany, the girl he'd dated in high school, had been the same way. As if beauty alone was all that mattered.

Whatever. He'd deal with her later. For now, he had work to do.

Keeping his foot planted on the accelerator, he pushed the speed limit, hoping there weren't any state patrol cars in the area. The sense of urgency to get to Cody was difficult to ignore.

As if sensing his tension, Royal pressed his nose against the wire mesh of the crate. Joel glanced at the dog using the rearview mirror. "Soon, boy. We'll be there soon."

Royal's tail thumped against the bottom of the crate in response.

Trina's home was a small ranch with light-green siding that looked as if it may have been there for decades. The yard was neatly tended. Flowery bushes framed the front door, and a water hose lay on the ground nearby. He pulled into the driveway and killed the engine. The front door opened as he slid out from behind the wheel, hitting the button to release the back hatch.

"Hi, Joel, it's good to see you again." Trina's expression was strained as she approached. She held a plastic bag in one hand. She stepped forward to envelop him in a friendly embrace. "Thank you for getting here so quickly."

"Of course." He hugged her back, then stepped to the side so Royal could jump down. He turned to face her. "Trina, will you please come closer?"

"Sure." She eyed him warily as she did so.

He knelt beside Royal and took Trina's hand. "Friend, Royal. Trina is a friend."

Royal sniffed her hand, then his tail wagged

from side to side. Trina's expression softened as she stroked the lab's soft, glossy black fur with her free hand. "You're a good boy, huh?"

"Yep." He smiled and rose to his feet. "As I said, Royal is very good at finding lost people. Is that Ben's clothing?"

"Yes." She handed the bag to him. "Dirty socks and T-shirts."

"Perfect. Give me a minute to get Royal ready." He pulled a fluorescent vest from the compartment beneath the crate and slipped it over Royal's torso. Then he filled a bowl with water and offered it to his K9.

Royal lapped the water, then lifted his head to stare up at him with large, expectant brown eyes.

"Are you ready? Huh, boy?" He injected enthusiasm into his tone to excite his dog. Searches were viewed as a game. The higher the play-and-prey drive in a K9, the better they performed. Shoving the collapsible bowl into the backpack, he shouldered the pack and opened the scent bag. "This is Ben. Ben! Search Ben!"

Royal buried his snout in the clothing, his tail wagging from side to side with anticipation. Then the lab whirled and began sniffing along the sidewalk.

"Ben's been living here with me since June," Trina said. "My sister passed away." Her brown eyes filled with grief. "I'm going through the process of formally adopting Ben, but he's not exactly thrilled to be here with me."

He nodded, his heart going out to her. It couldn't be easy to have a young boy dropped in your lap. "If he's not familiar with the area, he probably took a walk and got himself lost along the way."

"Maybe." She chewed her lower lip. "But I think he may have run away. He took his new backpack with him. When I was gathering his dirty clothes, I noticed some other things were missing, like his favorite handheld video game. The cabinet door was open, too, so he may have grabbed a snack."

"I see." He gestured toward Royal who sat at the front door and barked. "That's Royal's first alert. I need to reward him before we keep going."

Trina glanced at her watch, gnawing on her lip again. "Okay. But Ben's been gone now for over an hour."

"We'll find him." Joel empathized with her concern. He and his twin had run wild when they were eight, but that was because their parents had too many kids to watch them like hawks. And growing up on the dude ranch had given them free rein to do what they wanted. Yet he knew that wasn't how parents handled their kids these days. He was sure Ben had rarely been out of Trina's sight.

He hurried over to reward Royal with his stuffed

beaver. The dog leaped into the air to catch the beaver and ran around with the toy in his mouth. After a moment, he called the dog back and held out his palm. "Hand."

Royal regurgitated the stuffed beaver into his palm. Then he stared up at Joel, waiting for the next command.

"Search! Search Ben!"

Anxious to please, Royal turned and began sniffing around the yard. When the dog trotted around back, he quickly followed. Trina caught up, her gaze hopeful as she watched Royal work.

It didn't take long for Royal to head for the gap between the trees along the back of the yard. He glanced questioningly at Trina, who nodded.

"Yes, this is the shortcut to the hiking trail." She swallowed hard. "I checked both directions, calling out to Ben, but he didn't respond."

"Royal is on the scent." He wanted to reassure her they'd find Ben alive and unhurt, but he couldn't. He'd done too many of these search and rescue missions to know the outcome wasn't always positive.

Not that he had any intention of telling her that. Best to stay upbeat and confident. If the eight-year-old had decided to run away, by now he was probably tired, hungry, and more than ready to return home.

Royal turned north on the trail, his tail waving back and forth as the lab followed the scent. The trail went up a steep incline but eventually leveled off. He glanced at Trina. "Have you and Ben come this way before?"

"Never." She wrinkled her nose. "I suggested hiking, but Ben looked at me as if I had two heads. His mother died of a mountain biking accident, which might be part of the reason he turned me down. He's still grieving over his loss."

"Of course he is," Joel agreed. "It wasn't easy losing our parents when we were adults. It must be ten times harder for a child."

"I have him in counseling, but he tries to weasel out of attending his sessions." She sighed. "He makes me feel bad for insisting he go. I know it's for his own good, but he gets so angry with me."

"Yeah, well, anger is part of the grief process too." He looped his arm around her shoulders in a casual hug. "He'll come around."

"Will he?" She frowned and leaned against him for a moment, then pushed her hair from her face. "Sorry, it's just hard to know if I'm doing the right thing for him."

"You are." He squeezed her again, then released her. He watched as Royal continued on the path, then as he abruptly turned to the right. His K9 sniffed near a park bench, sat, and let out a sharp bark. "That's his alert!"

Trina broke away and ran toward Royal. "Ben? Where are you?"

Joel examined the park bench area, noticing there were blue and white sprinkle crumbs embedded in the dirt. "Do you think Ben took cookies of some kind?"

Trina frowned, spotting the sprinkles. Then her expression cleared. "Blueberry Pop-Tarts. He wanted them from the store, and while they're not exactly healthy, I gave in. The cupboard door was open this morning. I hadn't taken the time to see what he'd grabbed." She rubbed her eyes. "I'm glad he ate something."

"I agree, finding sprinkles is reassuring. Good boy, Royal! Good boy!" He tossed the stuffed beaver again. Royal sprinted after it.

"Your dog really can track his scent," she murmured. "I honestly wasn't convinced."

"A lot of people say that." He was used to the skeptics. "But our K9s are the real deal."

A faint smile tugged at the corner of her mouth. "Thanks. I owe you big time."

He waved that off. "The fee is a bag of dog food, if you can afford it. If not, don't worry, we tend to let the dog food fee slide when kids are involved."

"I can afford it." She raked her fingers through

her hair again. "I write books, which surprisingly do pretty well."

"Really?" He hadn't known that. He opened his mouth to ask more, but she held up her hand to stop him.

"Before you ask, no, I'm sure you haven't read any of them. I write cozy mystery books set in a small Montana town. My readers are mostly women, although I do have some male fans. But I'm sure they're not your type of story." She sighed, and added, "I was so glad I had a job that enabled me to work from home so I could be around for Ben, but that obviously hasn't worked. Ben still took off without telling me."

"It's not your fault." He could tell she believed it was. She was right that he wasn't a big reader, but he filed the information away for later. He didn't mind a good mystery. But now it was time to get back to work. "Here, Royal." He called his dog over and held out his hand for the beaver. "Search. Search Ben!"

Royal lowered his nose to the ground, but this time, rather than following the path, he trotted into the woods. Joel glanced at Trina, then followed his K9.

"This is why he got lost," Trina muttered. "Why didn't he stay on the path?"

"Maybe he saw an elk or deer." They weren't that

far from the Absaroka Mountains, home to all sorts of wildlife. "Kids that age are curious."

"Maybe." Trina didn't look reassured.

Royal continued moving along a curvy path through the woods. He could easily imagine an eight-year-old taking this route, around trees and over fallen logs. His K9 didn't hesitate or backtrack, so he knew Royal was still on the scent.

The longer they walked, the deeper the worry lines became etched in Trina's face. She gestured to a break in the trees. "The river isn't far from here. What if he fell in the water? I don't even know if Ben can swim! He has swim trunks, but that doesn't mean he can survive falling in the river!"

"Easy," he cautioned. "Royal will help us find him. Trust the process, okay?"

"I can't lose him," Trina whispered in a low, agonizing tone. "I just can't."

"Have faith in God," he encouraged. When she frowned, he realized she wasn't a believer. "I have faith, Trina. I believe God will watch over him."

"The way He watched over my sister, Evie?" Bitterness laced her tone. "Yeah, no thanks."

He decided to let it go. This wasn't the time to have this conversation. He kept his gaze focused on Royal's progress. He understood how difficult it was to get past anger and grief after losing a loved one. He and his eight siblings had struggled after losing their parents five and a half years ago. It was only after his parents had died in a plane crash that the siblings had gotten together and turned the former luxury dude ranch into a search and rescue operation.

They all lived on the ranch now, taking over the ten guest cabins. They each had their own space, but the siblings were also close at hand if needed. And their faith had grown stronger over the years.

Royal made another abrupt turn, this time heading away from the river. Joel reached over to grab Trina's hand when she stumbled while trying to keep up. "Are you okay?"

"Fine. I didn't expect that." She waved at the dog. "I was convinced he was heading to the river."

"This is why we stay back and let our K9 take the lead." He held her hand for a long moment, before releasing it. "We don't do anything to influence the dog one way or the other. Royal is following Ben's scent."

"I believe you, Joel, but where is he?" Trina sounded frustrated. "I don't see Ben anywhere."

He wasn't sure what to say because she was right. The hour was still early enough that there were no kids in the area. He saw a female jogger and an older man wearing a cowboy hat and using a walking stick, but even with the tourist season in full swing, the trail wasn't busy.

Then he saw a car driving past. There was too much foliage to see much, but he had to assume there was a road up ahead.

His spirits sank when Royal headed straight through the brush. When they came out on the other side, he saw the road. It appeared to lead to another subdivision.

Royal trotted faster now, sniffing along the side of the road.

"Auntie Trina!" The young voice came from around the corner of the street.

"Ben?" Trina sprinted forward. "Ben! I'm here!"

A young kid appeared around the corner, running toward them. Royal lifted his head and sniffed the air. Joel was about to call off the dog when a sharp crack of gunfire echoed through the area.

"Ben!" Trina pulled Ben close, curling her body over the boy, half carrying him to the shelter of the trees. Royal let out a sharp bark, either in warning to the gunman or to alert on his find.

Joel leaned over to grab Royal's vest, pulling the dog to the woods too. He crouched in front of Royal, Trina, and Ben and scanned the area. Long seconds turned into a full minute. Had that been a random gunshot?

Or were Trina and Ben in danger?

2

"Who's shooting?" Trina stared at Joel, trying to ascertain what had just happened. "Did you see him?"

"No." Joel scowled. "But stay down for a while, okay?"

She hugged Ben close. "It's okay. You're safe now."

Ben turned his face into her chest. Feeling the dampness of his tears tugged at her heart.

"I'm going to check the area," Joel said.

"Wait." She grabbed his arm. "What if the gunman is still out there?"

"It's been quiet." He shrugged, then rose to his feet. "Royal, search! Search for gold!"

Gold? She wanted to ask what that meant, but

Royal lifted his nose to the air and trotted out of the woods with Joel hot on his heels.

"I'm sorry," Ben whispered. "I shouldn't have run away."

She closed her eyes, relieved he was okay, then pressed a kiss to the top of his head. "I'm so glad you're not hurt. But, Ben, you can't just take off like that without telling me."

He lifted his tearstained face to hers. "I dreamed about Mom. I miss her so much . . ."

"Oh, Ben. I know you do." She pulled him close. "I miss her too. Please don't run away like this again. I'm here for you, Ben. We'll get through this to-gether, okay?"

He nodded against her. "Okay."

She leaned back, looking down at him. The gun-shot was concerning. "Did you see anyone while you were walking around?"

His slender shoulder lifted in a shrug, and he sniffled loudly. "A couple people. I didn't want them to see me, so I runned into the woods."

She nodded. Easy to see how his mind worked. He'd run away and hidden from people, only to get lost. Joel had been right about that part.

"You didn't see anyone familiar?" She tried to sound casual, but ever since hearing the gunfire, she'd wondered about Joel's father, Brian. Had her ex-brother-in-law changed his mind about being a father to Ben? It didn't make sense, but she didn't want to discount him from being involved either.

"No." He wiped his nose with his sleeve. "I'm hungry and thirsty."

"We'll get something to eat soon." She turned to see where Joel and Royal were. She felt certain the gunman was long gone but decided against moving from the shelter of the trees.

A moment later, Joel and Royal strode toward them. He wore a grim expression and had something tucked into his hand. He nodded at her. "I think the shooter is gone. We can head back to your place."

"What did you find?" She stood. Ben wiped his nose again, then stood too. She gently removed the backpack from the boy's shoulders to carry it for him. Ben glanced up at her, then eyed Royal curiously.

Joel hesitated, then said, "A shell casing."

Gold, she thought. That must have been what he meant by searching for gold. "Ben, this is Mr. Sullivan."

"Hi. Can I pet your dog?" Ben asked.

"Of course. Why don't you call me Joel." Joel knelt beside Royal. "Give me your hand, okay?"

Ben edged closer, extending his grimy hand. Joel

brought the small hand to Royal and addressed his K9 the same way he had with her. "Friend, Royal. Ben is a friend."

Royal sniffed the boy's hand, his tail wagging. Encouraged, Ben stepped closer and ran his fingers over Royal's glossy fur. "He's soft."

"Yes, especially behind his ears." Joel smiled gently as he knelt beside Royal and Ben. "Did you know Royal was following your scent? He was about to find you when you came rushing toward us."

"Really?" Ben's brown eyes, so like hers and Evie's, widened in amazement. "He can do that?"

"Yep. He's a very smart dog." Joel rose. "Come on, let's get out of here."

Trina was more than ready. She looped Ben's backpack over her shoulder and fell into step beside Joel. The gunfire continued to nag at her. Ben stayed close to her side, so she was afraid to say too much. "Any idea who fired the gun?"

Joel shook his head. "We'll talk to the Cody PD when we get back." He glanced down at Ben, then back at her. "Know of anyone who might be carrying a grudge?"

"No." She would have to explain about Brian later. "I'm sure it was some kid goofing around."

"Maybe." Joel's noncommittal response did not make her feel any better. He held up the small baggie containing the shell casing. "I'm hoping there will be fingerprints on this."

Seeing the brass up close made her shiver. What if this had been a targeted attempt to harm Ben? No, she couldn't believe that. Why would Brian or anyone want to hurt a child?

"Is there anyone in your life who may be upset with you?" Joel asked.

Her? She belatedly realized that possibility made far more sense than someone going after Ben. "I—no. Not really. I'm not seeing anyone now. Robby Rawlings and I broke up a few months ago." When Joel's blue eyes flared with keen interest, she shook her head. "No. Trust me, he found someone else. I hardly think he's upset with me."

"Who ended it?"

She flushed. "I did, but like I said, Robby has found someone else." She didn't want to mention the heated shouting match that had prefaced their breakup. Robby had a temper, but he'd never hit her the way Brian had struck out at Evie.

And she couldn't imagine him firing a gun at her, especially when Ben was close by. It would take a truly callous individual to do that.

Or someone foolish as to not understand the possible outcomes of their actions. Guns were everywhere in Wyoming. It was the rare person, like her, who didn't have one.

She personally didn't see the point. And she was glad she'd refrained from buying one now that she had Ben living with her.

"Who is Robby seeing?"

Joel's question interrupted her thoughts. "I don't know because I don't care." She shot him an exasperated look. "It's a moot point. We're not together, and he's not responsible for what happened back there."

"It's best to consider all possible theories." Joel clearly was not convinced. "What about other guys?"

She barely refrained from rolling her eyes. "You really expect me to name each of my three boyfriends? Seriously?"

"Yep." Joel arched a brow. "I told you, we need to cover all bases."

"Whatever." She put her hand on Ben's shoulder. "What would you like for breakfast?"

"Eggs and bacon?" Ben looked up at her hopefully, then his face fell. "I ate a Pop-Tart."

"I know. Royal found the park bench where you sat to eat. We also found blue and white sprinkles on the ground."

"Wow." Ben looked at Royal with admiration. "Can I share my breakfast with him?"

"No, Ben, you can't," Joel quickly interjected. "People food isn't healthy for him. And he won't eat anything unless I give it to him."

Ben frowned. "Why?"

"Because it's safer for our dogs if they don't eat anything they come across out in the wilderness," Joel patiently explained. "What if someone put spoiled food out and Royal ate it and got sick? We wouldn't want that, would we?"

Ben's eyes widened with horror. "No, I don't want Royal to get sick."

Joel nodded. "It's better if you play with him, instead of feeding him. Royal loves to play."

"Can I play with Royal, Aunt Trina?" Ben looked up at her with a gleam in his eyes. His fear over getting lost had eased. She was relieved he seemed to have survived the incident relatively un-scathed.

"Yes, after breakfast." She glanced at Joel. "You're welcome to stay."

Joel's expression softened. "I wouldn't mind. I fed Royal but left without eating anything other than a breakfast bar."

She was touched by his willingness to drop everything to help her find Ben. "Thank you, Joel."

"This is what we're trained for." He nodded toward Ben who had run ahead. "And finding Ben safe is all the reward I need."

"He apologized for running away, mentioned he'd dreamed about his mom." She sighed. "I wish there was something I could do to make this easier for him."

"Kids are resilient." Joel caught her hand, giving it a squeeze. "He'll come around. Starting school in a few weeks should help."

"I hope so." She thought about how Joel had mentioned having faith and believing that God would watch over her nephew. "I've been trying to get out more, to meet the neighbors, especially kids that are Ben's age. There's one boy, Mitch, who lives a few blocks from us. I've arranged for a few play-dates but need to find other kids too."

"I can imagine meeting the local kids wasn't part of your routine before now." Joel smiled. "I agree it's good to keep Ben busy."

"Yeah. Oh, good we're almost home." She gestured to the opening between two large trees. "I can't lie; my feet are killing me."

His low, husky chuckle sent a shiver of awareness down her spine. She tried to ignore it. This wasn't a good time for her old crush to resurface. Especially since she had Ben to worry about. Not only did she not have time for a relationship, but even if Joel was remotely interested, she suspected it wouldn't take him long to move on. He could get any girl he wanted. Her life was beyond boring.

Besides, Ben didn't need that sort of upheaval in his life. She had no intention of exposing him to a short-term relationship. The boy was dealing with enough as it was.

As they crossed through the trees to cross her backyard, Ben broke into a run. "Come play, Royal! Come play with me!"

"Go on, Royal." Joel gestured to the boy. The black lab quickly bounded after Ben.

Listening to Ben's laughter made her smile, lifting the heavy cloak of despair that had fallen over her while she'd searched for him.

She glanced up at the blue sky, wondering if maybe God had been watching over him after all.

Joel grabbed a tennis ball from his pack and handed it to Ben. "Throw this for him, he loves playing fetch."

"Okay." Ben threw the ball. It didn't go far, but Royal took off after it anyway. His K9 brought it back, dropped it at Ben's feet and looked up at the boy expectantly. Ben picked it up and threw it again.

Satisfied the boy would be preoccupied for a few minutes, he hastened to follow Trina inside. The house was nice, bigger than his cabin. She set Ben's backpack on the floor in the living room, then headed into the kitchen. As she pulled food items from the fridge, he crossed over to join her.

"Let's talk while Ben's outside. We need to call the Cody police, but I need to know about Ben's father." He held her gaze. "I assume he's not in the picture?"

"Correct. Brian and Evie divorced three years ago when Ben was five." She grimaced. "I don't think he paid any child support, and Evie didn't push the issue because she wanted sole custody. I can't imagine why Brian would show up here now, much less fire a gun at us."

"Maybe he's upset about you getting custody?"

"Why would he care? It's not like Evie had money or anything. There was barely a thousand dollars in her checking account, and she didn't have life insurance." She turned her back on him and began cracking eggs into a bowl. "I don't think someone fired at us on purpose. I'm sure it was kids goofing off. There's no reason to get the police involved. Ben is safe, and that's all that matters."

He frowned. "I would feel better getting this incident on record at the police station. Just in case something else happens. They might be able to lift a fingerprint from the brass Royal found."

"Later." She waved him off. "Ben's hungry. And so am I."

Swallowing a sigh, he let it go. She could be right about the gunfire being from a kid. He and Royal had scouted the area without finding anyone lurking nearby. Just the shell casing, which may or may not help find the gunman.

"Do you mind if I make coffee?" He gestured toward the coffee maker.

"That would be great." She smiled weakly as she whisked the eggs together. "I'm usually on my second or third cup by now."

"Same." He went to work, thinking again about the shooting incident. That anyone would be careless with a firearm near a child bothered him.

That alone was worth reporting to the police. Even if it had been some teen goofing off, the kid needed a stern talking to.

Looking out the window as he waited for the coffee to brew, he watched as Royal chased the ball for Ben. The kid was grinning from ear to ear, giving Joel hope that the boy would find a way to get past his grief. He knew from experience there would be good days and bad ones.

But over time, the heartache lessened. At least he and his siblings had been able to fall back on their faith.

It bothered him that Trina had seemingly turned away from God.

"I know you don't want to hear this, but it may help Ben to know his mother is looking down on him from heaven." He chose his words carefully. "I know that helped us after our parents died. We took some comfort in knowing they were together."

She shot him a quick look, then shrugged. "I'll consider that, thanks."

He wanted to push the issue but reminded himself that Ben wasn't his son or his responsibility. Joel's experience with women wasn't great, and he'd pretty much soured on the whole idea of marriage. His older siblings had been dropping like flies, which had only reinforced his determination to stay away from the marriage scene.

Yet he had to admit that the spouses his siblings had chosen blended into their family very well. Maybe if he'd found someone like that . . .

But he hadn't. And being burned a few times made it less likely that he ever would.

When the coffee finished, he poured two cups, handing a mug to Trina.

"Thanks." She had strips of bacon frying in a pan. "I should have asked if scrambled eggs are okay. They're Ben's favorite."

"I'm not picky." He was hungry enough to eat just about anything. "I can take over making the bacon." He nudged her side, then nodded toward the window. "Looks like Ben and Royal are tired out."

She moved out of the way, her expression softening when she noticed Ben lying on the grass with Royal stretched out beside him. "Ben looks so happy and carefree. It's as if his bad dream and running away had never happened. Maybe I need to get him a dog."

"Good idea." He grinned. "Dogs are great companions."

She playfully elbowed him in the ribs. "Sure, that's one way of looking at it. The other side is that dogs need constant attention. You know as well as I do I'll be the one doing all the work taking care of it, feeding it, and cleaning up after it."

"I understand, but you should also make sure Ben chips in to help. He looks happy with Royal out there. And trust me, the effort of taking care of an animal is well worth it." He wasn't lying about that. He wouldn't change having Royal as his K9 SAR partner for anything.

"I'll look into it." She opened the cupboard to grab plates. After setting them on the table, she went to the front door. "Ben! Breakfast is almost ready."

Still able to see the boy through the window, Joel watched as the boy rolled over onto his stomach, giggling when Royal licked his cheek. More proof, in his humble opinion, that Ben would benefit from a pet.

He flipped the strips of bacon until they were nice and crispy. Then he reached over and began the scrambled eggs. His family had Anna to help coordinate their searches and cook meals, but his parents had made sure each of the Sullivan siblings could cook. And do laundry. Not to mention the multitude of other ranch chores.

There had been times when he'd resented the work, but looking back, he could appreciate his upbringing. The hard work they'd done as kids had transformed into their dedication and determination to succeed in their search and rescue missions as adults.

"Go into the bathroom to wash your hands," Trina said.

"Why?" Ben's voice was whiny. "They're not dirty."

"You probably have Royal's saliva all over them from throwing the ball." He glanced over his shoulder, smiling to note his K9 had stretched out on the floor under the table. That was a typical place for their dogs to be when they were eating in restaurants. Royal must have decided this was a similar situation.

Ben frowned, stared down at his hands for a moment, then hurried down the hall toward the bathrooms. Trina arched a brow. "Thanks, but really, I'd like him to listen to me, not you."

"Sorry, I was just pointing out the obvious." He finished making the scrambled eggs. "I'll stay out of it next time. I need a platter."

Trina opened another cupboard and handed it to him. He piled the scrambled eggs and bacon strips on the wide plate and carried it to the table.

A moment later, Ben ran back into the room. "No doggie germs, see?"

The wash job wasn't great, but he wasn't about to mention it. Trina didn't either.

"Sit down, Ben." She picked up the platter and spooned a serving of eggs and bacon onto his plate.

Joel carried his coffee to the table and took the empty seat on the other side of Ben. "If you don't mind, I'd like to say grace."

Trina froze for a moment, then nodded. She filled her plate, then pushed the platter toward him. She sat and bowed her head.

"What's grace?" Ben asked.

"A prayer. Like this," Joel said. "Dear Lord Jesus, we thank You for this wonderful food we're about to eat. We ask that You continue to keep us all safe in Your care. Amen."

Another pause, then Trina echoed, "Amen."

"Jesus didn't make the food," Ben protested. "You and Aunt Trina did."

"That's true, but Jesus has blessed us with the ability to buy and make food, so it's only right that we thank Him for it." He wondered if all kids were so literal. "Someday I'll tell you the story of Jesus."

"Okay." Ben shrugged and took a bite of his bacon.

"We should be the ones thanking you, Joel." Trina subtly changed the subject. "How many search and rescue calls do you get each month?"

"In the summer? A lot." He took a bite of his eggs. "For some reason, this has been an unusually busy season for us."

"Maybe more people are taking road trips rather than opting for more expensive vacations," she suggested.

"Could be. We've had days where we're all out on calls at the same time." He shook his head. "That hasn't happened before."

"I'm sorry to contribute to your workload." Trina glanced at Ben, then added, "Please tell me which brand of dog food you use."

He hesitated, then nodded and gave her the information. His parents had put their massive investments in a trust prior to their death. He and his siblings hadn't known how much money they had and thankfully had been able to keep the extent of their wealth a secret. The Sullivan K9 Ranch took a significant amount of money to run, not to mention the upkeep of their vehicles, the K9s, and their horses. They paid an exorbitant amount for veterinary bills. They each drew a modest salary; the bulk of the investments were saved for running the ranch.

For a moment, he imagined Ben playing with Chase and Wynona's son, Eli, goofing around with the dogs, and maybe riding horses. Then he abruptly dismissed the idea. His job here was done. Ben would be fine. His getting lost this morning might have helped the boy appreciate the home his aunt provided for him.

And it was obvious Trina cared about the little boy.

So what if he admired her determination to raise her sister's child? He would not hesitate to do the same for his siblings.

Joel quickly finished his breakfast, then drained his coffee. "Delicious," he said. "Thanks Trina. I need to get back to the ranch."

"Can Royal stay with us for a while?" Ben asked. His pleading gaze was hard to resist.

"No, Ben, Royal has more lost people to find." Trina reached over to smooth her hand over Ben's back. "You wouldn't want others to be lost, too, right?"

"I guess." Ben sneaked a piece of bacon off his plate and held it under the table. Joel pretended not to notice as he carried his dirty dishes to the sink. He was confident Royal wouldn't take the bait, but he wanted to prove it to Ben.

When he turned back to the table, Ben was staring under the table at Royal. Then he shot Joel a guilty look. "I was just testing him."

He fought the urge to smile, keeping his expression serious. "I don't want you to do that, Ben. It's not fair to Royal to be teased with something he can't have. You wouldn't want me to eat ice cream in front of you, would you?"

"No." Ben scowled and stared at the floor for a minute. "But a small bite of bacon can't hurt."

"It can hurt him," Joel said, trying to be patient. "People food isn't good for dogs. He might get sick, and what if he eats something that's really bad for him? Did you know that a dog like Royal could die if he ate chocolate?"

Ben's eyes widened in horror. "Why?"

"Because it contains substances that are toxic for dogs. Royal wouldn't be able to digest some of the ingredients in chocolate, so it would make him super sick to the point he could die." He gave the boy a stern look. "I need you to promise you won't try to feed him anymore, okay?"

"Okay." Ben quickly popped the piece of bacon into his mouth. "Sorry," he mumbled around the food.

"Thank you." He glanced over at Trina who looked weary. He could only imagine how difficult it would be to become the guardian of an eight-year-old overnight. The kid was either questioning everything or pushing the boundaries. He crossed over to rest his hand on her shoulder, silently reassuring her she was doing a great job. "Come, Royal." The lab crawled out from beneath the table. He stroked the dog, then moved toward the door. "Take care, Trina. I'll see you around."

She quickly jumped up and crossed over to join him. "Thanks again, Joel." Then as he was about to step out, she surprised him by drawing him in for a hug. "I appreciate everything you and Royal have done for us."

He held her close for a moment, then stepped back. "My pleasure." As search and rescue calls went, this had been one of the better ones. He'd take a good outcome over a bad one any day of the week.

Before he could head outside, another sharp crack of gunfire ripped through the air. He instinctively ducked, throwing himself over Trina who was beside him.

He quickly backed away from the opening, drawing Trina with him and making sure that Royal was still inside too.

Then he slammed the door and shot the dead bolt home. "Get Ben into the bathroom and stay down away from the windows, understand?"

She stared at him, then wordlessly nodded. "Come, Ben. Hurry."

He moved to the window and searched for the shooter. He didn't see anyone, but there was no way he was leaving now. He pulled out his phone to dial 911.

A second round of gunfire in a matter of hours was not a coincidence. Someone wanted to harm Trina and Ben.

And he wasn't leaving until he knew they were safe.

3

"What's going on?" Ben asked fearfully. She'd drawn him into the bathtub where they hunkered down to wait.

Trina hesitated, unsure of what to say. She didn't want to scare him any more than was necessary. "I think there must be some kids goofing around with guns outside. We're going to call the police to make sure they stop."

"Guns are not a toy," Ben said solemnly, clearly having heard this phrase from an adult at some point in his life. Where, she wasn't sure. Had Brian bought a gun? Evie didn't have one at least, not in the apartment Trina had cleared out after her death.

"No, they are not." She tried to smile. "We're safe here. Joel and Royal will make sure of that. We're just being extra careful."

"I love Royal," Ben announced. "I want him to live with us forever."

She suppressed a sigh. "Royal lives with Joel on their ranch, so you can't live with him. I'll look into getting a puppy, okay? I'm sure Joel will have an idea where we can find one."

"Really?" Ben's big brown eyes held hers. "A puppy of my own?"

"Yes." She would probably regret agreeing to this, but the shining joy in Ben's eyes was worth the extra work. And maybe Joel was right about giving Ben some responsibility. Playing with a puppy would distract him from his video games and maybe ease his grief over losing his mother.

"Will our puppy search for people too?" Ben asked. Now that she'd mentioned the dog, he seemed to have a one-track mind. Which was good because she didn't want him focused on the gunfire.

What was going on with that anyway? She'd hoped the original gunshot was from irresponsible kids, but now she wasn't so sure.

Realizing Ben was waiting for her answer, she shook her head. "I don't think so, Ben. Doing that takes hours and hours of training. You'll be too busy when school starts in a few weeks for that."

"You can do it," Ben said. "You have lots of time."

"We'll see." These past few months with Ben had helped her understand why parents said vague things like, *We'll see.* Kids could be incredibly persistent. "I have to work at my computer, remember? That's how I get paid."

"I know." Ben shrugged that off as if it were a nonissue. "It would be so cool to have a dog that can track people."

So now a puppy alone wasn't good enough? She tried not to sigh.

The wail of police sirens filled her with relief. Hopefully, the Cody police officers would be able to find the person who had recklessly fired their weapon. It was still difficult to believe that someone hated her enough to do such a thing.

Her previous boyfriends hadn't cared enough to lash out at her. Robby was the only one who'd seemed angry when she'd broken things off, but he hadn't wasted any time in finding another girl either.

Yet now that there had been two shooting incidents, she needed to consider all possibilities. Joel had been right about that.

Could Brian be involved? Or Evie's most recent boyfriend, Peter Thomas? Her sister had a knack for dating the wrong kind of guys. *Not that my track record is much better*, she silently admitted.

"Trina? You and Ben can come out now," Joel called through the door.

"Okay." She rose on shaky knees and stepped over the edge of the tub. Ben quickly followed suit.

When she opened the bathroom door, Royal was there to greet them. Ben instantly went down on his knees to hug the dog. Royal licked Ben, his tail thumping against the wall. She realized Joel had sent Royal on purpose.

Leaving Ben and Royal, she headed into the kitchen. Two Cody police officers stood beside Joel. She recognized the older cop, Burt Jones, from an incident that had taken place back in high school. The other one she didn't know.

"Trina, this is Officer Burt Jones and Officer Heath Anderson." Joel made the quick introductions. "We have reason to believe Trina Warren is being targeted."

"Do you have any idea who has a grudge against you?" Jones asked.

"No, I really don't." It would be easier if she did. "I can give you the names of my previous boyfriends, but I find it hard to imagine them doing this."

Joel shot her an impatient look. "Trina has recently been given guardianship over her nephew, Ben. His father could be responsible."

"His name is Brian Ashland." She glanced over her shoulder to make sure Ben wasn't paying attention. "He and my sister divorced three years ago, when Ben was five. I don't think Ben has seen his father since then. My sister, Evie, legally changed Ben's last name to Warren."

"Brian Ashland?" Officer Anderson repeated. "Last known address?"

"Um." She searched her memory. "They lived in an apartment on Oakdale Street in Laramie. I can't remember the building number. My sister moved out of there when they separated."

"Laramie, huh?" Burt Jones scowled. "That means we have to work with the Laramie PD to find him."

"My sister was also dating a guy, Peter Thomas, prior to her death. He lives in Laramie too." She shrugged. "I never met him, and as far as I know, he'd have no reason to shoot me."

"What about your ex-boyfriends?" Joel arched a brow. "They're local, aren't they?"

"Yes." She swallowed a sigh and turned toward the officers. "Robby Rawlings, Toby Silver, and Luke Davenport." She felt foolish naming them since she did not for one minute believe they were involved.

Yet Joel clearly wouldn't be satisfied until they'd been ruled out.

Officer Heath Anderson made notes. "Okay, did you notice anyone hanging around recently?"

She flushed. When she wasn't in her office working, she cared for Ben—cooking, cleaning, and laundry along with trying to bond with the boy. She'd even learned how to play his favorite video game. But to her shame, she hadn't paid attention to their surroundings. Even if she'd have seen someone outside, she probably wouldn't have thought much about it.

As Ben's guardian, she needed to do better. "No, I haven't."

"As I mentioned earlier, Ben ran away this morning." Thankfully, Joel changed the subject. "He took his backpack and some snacks and headed up the hiking trail. Royal helped find him, and that was when the first incident of gunfire occurred. The second taking place here at the house can't be a coincidence."

"I agree," Heath said. Burt nodded in agreement. "We'll ask around; hopefully, someone saw something." The officer pinned her with a stern look. "You need to be careful from here on out. If you notice anyone lingering nearby, call us right away."

Her mouth went dry as she realized what he was really saying. That she and Ben could truly be in danger. "I will."

"I'll be taking Ms. Warren and Ben to a hotel," Joel said. "They're not staying here until we know who is behind these attempts."

She frowned. "We can't leave. I have work to do."

Joel narrowed his gaze. "You have a laptop computer, don't you? Staying here is not an option. Whoever took that shot is likely to come back."

A chill ran down her spine. She had convinced herself this was the work of irresponsible kids. But if not?

Ben ran around the room, giggling when Royal followed. One look at her nephew made her realize Joel was right.

They couldn't stay here.

Catching Joel's gaze, she reluctantly nodded. "Okay. I'll pack our things."

"Thank you." Joel turned back toward the officers. "I'll give you our contact information. Will you please call us with updates regarding your investigation?"

The officers exchanged a long look, then Heath Anderson nodded. "Sure thing."

Leaving Joel to provide their cell numbers, she turned toward the bedrooms to pack a bag for herself and Ben.

Hopefully, finding the person responsible wouldn't take too long. She knew without being told Joel wasn't heading back to the ranch until they'd caught this guy.

And the last thing she needed was to spend time with the man she'd secretly admired since the eleventh grade.

~

JOEL BLEW out a breath in frustration. Oh, it wasn't that he didn't trust the Cody police to do their job, it was just a matter of how long that would take.

As he'd told Trina, summer was their busiest time. Being out of commission even for a day or two could put a crimp in their ability to help their community.

He stepped aside to make a quick call to Anna, the Sullivan housekeeper, general manager, and beloved family friend. "I need to stay in Cody for a while. You'll need to take me and Royal out of the rotation."

"Are you in danger?" Anna asked with concern.

Since he knew he'd get an earful from his oldest brother, Chase, if he mentioned the episodes of gunfire, he kept that part to himself. "I'm not in danger. I'm just helping a friend."

"Are you sure?" Anna sounded suspicious.

"I'm positive." He wasn't lying exactly because Trina was the gunman's target. "Let Chase and Maya know I'll be in touch later."

"Okay, be careful, Joel." Anna ended the call without saying anything more.

Pocketing his phone, he glanced out the window to where Jones and Anderson were walking the neighborhood. He wished he'd noticed if anyone was outside, but his attention had been diverted by Trina's warm embrace.

She'd hugged him as a friend, nothing more. Which was good since he wasn't interested in anything more. Even if he was, a ready-made family wouldn't be high on his list.

Better that he stay focused, on alert for signs of danger. No matter what Trina said, he felt certain she was the target. Not to brag, but most people in the area admired his family for the work they did. Maybe there were rare exceptions when they got involved in dangerous situations, but overall, he never worried about someone coming after him or his siblings.

Ben came over to stand beside him. "Can I go outside to play with Royal again?"

He hid a wince. "Not right now, sorry." He glanced up as Trina entered the kitchen, pulling a rolling suitcase behind her. "We're going to stay at a hotel for a while."

Ben cocked his head to the side. "Why?"

"Ah, because we thought it would be fun." He glanced helplessly at Trina who shrugged as if to say she had no idea how to approach this either. He racked his brain for a moment, then remembered the Elk Lodge had an indoor pool. "We'll see if we can stay at a place with a pool. Do you like to swim?"

Trina looked surprised by that, but Ben instantly responded, "Yay! A pool! I wanna swim. Can we, Aunt Trina?"

"Of course. Give me a minute to grab your swimming suit." She hurried from the room, returning a few minutes later with the garment.

"Goody." Ben's eyes glowed with anticipation. "Does Royal know how to swim?"

"He does," Joel said. "He's a black lab, and labs generally like the water."

"Aunt Trina, can we get a lab like Royal?" Ben asked. "I wanna take him swimming with me."

"We'll see." Trina had shoved the swimming trunks into the suitcase, then gestured toward the bedrooms. "I need a minute to grab my laptop."

He took the rolling suitcase to the door. "Ben, I need you to stay here with Royal."

"Okay." Ben grinned. "I'm glad Royal is going with us."

Joel took the suitcase out to his SUV that he'd left parked at the curb. As he tucked the luggage into the back seat, he glanced around. The hour was still early enough that there weren't many people out and about. There were houses on either side of Trina's, but they weren't so close as to infringe on her privacy.

A fact that worked against her now that she'd been targeted by a gunman.

He closed the door and headed back up to the house. Leaving for a few days was the right thing to do. Yet he couldn't deny the sense of unease that dogged his footsteps.

Should he ask his DEA brother-in-law, Doug Bridges, for help? Or his sister's new fiancé, FBI Agent Griffin Flannery?

He'd give the local cops some time to see what they came up with. If they couldn't make headway on the case, he'd call his family. While both Doug and Griff were decent guys, they were still federal agents. Calling them for help now would be akin to spitting in the local cops faces.

Entering the kitchen, he found Trina stuffing snacks into her laptop case. She shrugged when she saw him. "Kids are always hungry," she explained.

"Totally get that." He reached for the case. "We'll take my car; it has a crate area for Royal, along with extra supplies."

She nodded and turned to Ben. "Ready to go?"

"Yeah." Ben jumped up from the floor. "I wanna sit in the back with Royal."

"Royal has to stay in his crate area." Joel held the door open for them, again sweeping his gaze over the area. The police cruisers were parked in the street, so he felt certain the gunman wouldn't try again.

"Why?" Ben asked.

"It's safer for Royal to be back there. Besides, he likes it." Joel's experience with kids was limited to Chase's recently turned five-year-old son, Elijah, who was not talkative at all. The family had to constantly remind Eli to use his words to express what he wanted.

In contrast, Ben talked nonstop, and his favorite word appeared to be *why*.

"Enough, Ben," Trina said when it looked as if the kid would argue. "We're not going far, so be patient. You'll have time with Royal soon enough."

Ben heaved a sigh but, thankfully, let it go.

Once they were settled in the SUV, Joel put the vehicle in gear and headed to the Elk Lodge. It was the nicest hotel in the city, which didn't make it a five-star establishment by any stretch of the imagination, but it would work well for their needs. His siblings had used the place on occasion, and he knew they had suites available.

The indoor pool was a bonus.

"I hope the police find the person responsible soon." Trina kept her voice down as if hoping Ben wouldn't hear.

A glance in his rearview mirror confirmed Ben was wiggling his fingers through the wires of the crate area. Royal licked them, making the boy laugh.

"I'm sure they will. And if not, I can call my family for help." He flashed a reassuring smile. "My brother-in-law Doug Bridges is a federal agent, and my sister Alexis is engaged to Griffin Flannery who works for the FBI."

"Wow." She looked impressed. "I had no idea."

He shrugged. "Some people don't like the federal government, but they're good at their jobs and have helped solve more than one crime in recent months."

"Like what?"

"Alexis and Griff recently arrested a serial killer." He looked at her in surprise. "You didn't hear about that?"

"Oh yeah, I sort of remember that." Her cheeks went pink. "I was moving a bunch of Ben's stuff from Laramie to my house at the time. Things have been chaotic since my sister's passing."

"That's understandable." No doubt settling things in Laramie and moving Ben to his new home had been a monumental task. "I'm just saying, if the police can't help, we'll call in the big guns."

A reluctant smile tugged at the corner of her mouth. "Sounds good to me."

Joel tried not to notice how pretty Trina was, especially when she smiled. Rather than heading straight to the Elk Lodge, he made several turns just to make sure they weren't being followed.

Seeing nothing suspicious, he drove to the hotel.

"Will having Royal stay in the room with us be a

problem?" Trina asked when he pulled into the parking lot.

"Nope." He grinned. "Everyone here knows our K9s are well trained."

"Probably better than some kids," she joked, reaching for her laptop case. "I hope they'll let us in early."

He did too. Nine thirty in the morning wasn't the usual check-in time, but he didn't mind paying extra if needed. He opened the back hatch for Royal, then reached into the back seat for the rolling suitcase.

Ben bent to pet Royal the moment the dog jumped out of the back. The three of them together, along with his K9, walked into the hotel lobby. A large stone fireplace lined one wall, and a sofa and two stuffed chairs faced it. Being August, there wasn't a fire. There were a couple of people sitting there, looking at them curiously as they walked past. Joel was conscious of the fact that they looked like a family but quickly shoved that image aside.

"We'd like a suite please," he said to the clerk. "I know it's early, but I'm happy to pay for an early check-in."

"Let's see what we have." The young man tapped on the computer. "You're in luck. Looks like there's a two-bedroom suite available."

"We'll take it." He reached for his wallet, but Trina was faster.

"I've got this." She pushed her credit card across the counter.

"Trina, I'm more than willing to pay," he began.

"No thank you." Her tone was firm. "I'm the reason we're here, remember?"

Since that was true, he felt forced to let it go. It didn't sit well with him to have her pay, but at the same time, he found Trina's stubborn independence attractive.

He didn't mind paying for dinner, movies, or other social outings when he was dating a woman. In fact, he insisted on it. Yet Bethany had acted as if she were doing him a favor by going out with him, as if men in general should bow to her every wish. He'd suspected Lisa was the same way, which was why he'd kept his distance. He assumed their attitude was in part because they were strikingly beautiful and believed they could have any man they wanted.

Yet conversely, when he'd broken things off with Bethany, she'd gotten upset with him. And when he'd declined to date Lisa, she'd been the same way. He thought their behavior was odd. It wasn't as if there were a shortage of men in the area, but they'd still been upset with him.

And that was why he was out of the dating scene.

He stood back, watching Ben talk to Royal as

Trina finished the registration process. Ben backed into the suitcase. Joel grabbed it before it could fall to the floor.

"I wanna play outside with Royal," Ben whined.

"I thought you wanted to swim?" Joel accepted the room key Trina handed him.

"Come on, Ben." Trina leveled the boy with a stern look. "You'll have plenty of time to play with Royal. How about we check out the pool, okay?"

Ben brightened. "Okay."

Crisis averted, Joel thought as he pulled the suitcase and Trina's computer bag down the hallway toward the suite. He knew from previous visits that the suites had first-floor access to the outside, which was helpful in taking care of a dog.

The suite was nice. Trina headed to the bedroom on the right, which housed two queen beds. "This is our room, Ben." She smiled gratefully when he hoisted the suitcase onto the bed. "Let's find your swimming trunks."

"I need to get stuff out of the SUV for Royal," he told her. "I'll be back in a few."

Leaving her to Ben, he took Royal outside with him. "Get busy," he told the K9. That was the term they used for encouraging the dogs to relieve themselves. Maya had started the phrase when she'd worked on the Cheyenne police force with a K9 partner. Her dog had been killed in the line of duty shortly before their parents had died. Maya had brought in a world-renowned dog trainer so they could begin their search and rescue services. And they'd all named their K9s after national parks.

"Good boy," he praised, cleaning up after his K9. "You're a good boy."

His black lab wiggled with excitement. Joel grabbed a pail of dog food and his duffel containing a clean pair of clothes. He and his siblings always packed for an emergency.

"Let's go, Royal." He led the way inside.

When he reached the suite, though, he was surprised to see Ben was crying.

"What happened?" He'd have thought the idea of swimming would have been enough of a distraction.

"He left his favorite video game in his backpack." Trina looked frazzled. "He took it with him this morning, and I forgot about it when I packed our stuff."

"I want my game," Ben whined, tears rolling down his cheeks. "Please, Auntie Trina, can we go back to get it?"

She sighed. "Let's wait until after we swim."

The boy wore swim trunks and a T-shirt, but that wasn't good enough. "No! Now. I want my game now."

"Stop it, Ben." Trina's tone was sharp. "That's not how you ask for a favor."

Ben threw himself onto the sofa. Royal trotted over to lick him in the face.

After a moment, Ben sat up, rubbing his face. "Aunt Trina, can we please go back to get my game?"

"That's better." She glanced wearily at Joel. "Do you mind?"

"No problem." He would have offered to run the errand himself, but he didn't like the idea of leaving them there alone. "Let's go. It won't take long."

Ben scrambled to his feet, shoving his feet into his shoes. Joel eyed him. "What do you say?"

Ben looked confused for a moment, then said, "Thank you."

Joel nodded and led the way back outside. Moments later, they were back in the SUV heading west.

"I should have double-checked before leaving the house," Trina said. "I knew he'd taken his favorite video game with him this morning."

"Hey, it's fine. Kids, you know?" He brushed it off. "At least he didn't notice this at bedtime."

"Right?" Trina laughed, the tension easing from her expression.

He frowned when he noticed a plume of black smoke in the distance. Most people didn't use fireplaces or wood-burning stoves in August. And it was too early for burning leaves or other debris.

When they reached the next intersection, he heard sirens. Could the smoke be from a house fire?

He increased his speed, battling a sense of dread. When he turned into the subdivision where Trina's house was located, his eyes widened in horror when he saw Trina's front door was engulfed in flames.

"Joel! My house is on fire!"

He pulled over to the side of the road and threw the gearshift into park. "Stay here." He bolted out from the SUV and ran to where he'd seen a garden hose earlier that day.

Praying the rest of the fire department would get there in time to save Trina's home.

4

How had this happened? Trina stared in horror at the yellow fingers of flames crawling up and around the front door of her house, trying to pry their way inside. Had someone tossed a cigarette onto her front porch that had started the blaze? The past week had been unusually dry, no rain for almost ten days. Yet as she watched Joel use the hose on the house to douse the flames, she knew that wasn't it.

The fire had been set on purpose. Likely by the same person who'd taken shots at her. But why? That was the part she didn't understand. Ben's father Brian? What did he gain from doing something like that?

"Aunt Trina, what's going on?" Ben's voice had her turning in her seat to look at him. He'd been so preoccupied with Royal when they'd pulled up that he hadn't noticed the fire. But now his eyes were wide with fear.

"It looks like there's a small fire." She had no idea how much to tell him. The last thing she wanted was for him to be scared to death that something bad would happen to him, the way it had taken his mother. The shrill sirens grew louder, so she had to raise her voice to be heard. "Don't worry, Joel has the hose going, see? The fire is almost out. Everything will be fine."

Ben's expression was troubled, but he didn't ask anything more. His attention was diverted by the long red fire truck that passed them, coming to a stop directly in front of her home. Joel continued working with her garden hose as firefighters bailed from the truck and ran forward to assist.

The fire truck hoses were huge, and soon the firefighters had gotten Joel out of the way to take over fighting the blaze. After a moment, he returned to the car. His grim expression proved her assumption that the fire was set on purpose was correct.

"The front door was doused with gasoline." He shot a quick glance at Ben who was clearly listening. "Thankfully, we caught it early, all because we came back to get Ben's video game. I'm hoping the damage won't be too bad."

She nodded. Her throat tightened as the realization sank deep. Arson was a big deal. Even if the damage was limited to the front door of the house, the water used to put the fire out could be a problem too.

"I helped?" Ben asked.

"Yes, you did," Joel assured him. "But I'm sorry to say we won't be able to go inside to get your game."

Ben frowned, then glanced at her. "That's okay."

She wanted to hug him for being so understanding. "Thank you, Ben. We'll get your game another time."

"The police are here." Joel gestured to the squad that pulled up next to the fire truck. "They'll want to talk to you, Trina."

She didn't know any more than the last time they'd questioned her about the gunfire, but she nodded and pushed out of the SUV. The acrid scent of smoke was overwhelming. She stood waiting, but the two officers split up and walked the area. It took a moment to realize they were making sure the person who'd done this wasn't hanging around nearby.

She glanced around with apprehension. What if the killer was out there watching her? Her neighbors typically worked during the day. Eyeing the properties on either side of her home, she didn't see anyone peering through the windows or standing on the porch gawking.

And that meant nobody had likely seen the person who'd set the fire either.

After a few minutes of walking the street, Burt Jones and Heath Anderson crossed over to her.

"The preliminary report is that this is arson. Sometimes fire bugs like to stay close to watch things burn." Burt's expression was grave. "Any idea who could have done this?"

"The same person who'd taken shots at me, but I can't imagine why he switched from firing a gun to starting a fire." She swallowed hard. "I'm grateful we weren't home when the fire was started."

"Yeah, I thought Sullivan was taking you away from here?" Heath asked.

"We're staying at a hotel in town but came back for Ben's video game." She gestured to the house as Joel slid out of the driver's seat to join them. "Joel used the hose to douse the flames prior to the fire department showing up."

"The gasoline scent was very strong," Joel added. "No question in my mind that this was arson."

Burt and Heath eyed each other somberly.

"We called the Laramie PD to request information on your sister's ex-husband, Brian Ashland." Burt grimaced. "They haven't responded yet."

"Based on this, we'll call them again," Heath

said with a dark frown. "We need to know where this guy is ASAP."

She was grateful they were taking the threat seriously, even though she really couldn't imagine Brian doing such a thing. Granted, he had struck Evie in anger, but that was different from this level of rage.

It was terrifying to have this much fury directed at her.

"We'll check into your sister's boyfriend too. Peter Thomas, right?" When she nodded, Burt continued, "At this point, everyone is a suspect until we can rule them out."

She tried to remain positive. Burt and Heath were good cops. She knew they'd do everything possible to get to the bottom of this.

"We need you to keep thinking about other possible suspects." Heath gestured to the house. "This guy knows where you live, so he must be someone familiar with you."

"Other than the three boyfriend names I gave you, Robbie Rawlings, Toby Silver and Luke Davenport, I can't think of anyone else who would stoop to this level." To her mind, even her previous boyfriends were a stretch.

In truth, there weren't as many women as there were men in Cody, which is likely the main reason each of the three men had asked her out in the first place. She knew she wasn't any guy's first choice. She wasn't pretty or outgoing.

Quite the opposite. Prior to taking custody of Ben, there had been several days she'd never changed out of her pajamas, especially when she was lost in one of her stories. That was the biggest perk of working from home.

"Do you need anything else?" A hint of impatience underscored Joel's tone. "I'd like to get Ben and Trina back to the hotel."

"Go ahead." Burt waved a hand. "We'll be in touch if we learn anything new."

Trina frowned. "What about my house?" The idea of driving away didn't sit well with her. "What if the arsonist comes back?"

"Good point. I'll talk to our sergeant about having an officer keep an eye on the place," Heath offered. "Our resources are limited, but this is an extreme case. Maybe we can get someone in plain clothes to hide nearby. That way we can arrest him if he does come back."

"That's a great idea." Joel flashed a reassuring smile. "I like the idea of this guy getting caught sooner rather than later."

"We'll canvass the neighborhood," Heath added. "Hopefully, someone noticed a car parked nearby or someone hauling a gasoline can toward the house."

"Maybe check gas station video to see if anyone

filled a gas can recently," Joel suggested. "I know people use them for lawn mowers, but it might give you a starting point."

"Yeah, that's a strong possibility." Burt looked thoughtful. "If you think of anything else, let us know."

Trina wondered if Joel would mention his brother-in-law the federal agent or the other brother-in-law who was with the DEA, but he didn't.

"You'll want to let your insurance company know about this." Heath gestured to the house. "They'll want to send someone out to assess the damage."

"Okay, thank you." She made a mental note to make the call sooner than later.

One of the firefighters jogged over. "Ms. Warren?"

"Yes?" She took a step toward him. "Is the fire out?"

"Yes, ma'am." He nodded at Joel. "Thanks to the quick work of Sullivan here, we believe the damage has been mitigated. The fire mostly involved the front door of the property. I'm afraid your flower bushes may not survive. It's hard to know how much gasoline was used around the front door, and it looks some of the fuel seeped into the earth."

She'd enjoyed those flower bushes, but they were the least of her worries. "I understand."

The firefighter gave her a nod and turned away. She blew out a breath and focused on her blessings.

She and Ben were fine, and her house wasn't a complete loss. The fire shouldn't have happened, but it could have been so much worse.

"Are you okay?" Joel eyed her over the hood of the car.

"I guess." She slid into the passenger seat, pulling the door closed behind her.

"What did the police say?" Ben asked. "Did they arrest the bad guy?"

"Not yet, but soon." She forced herself to sound upbeat. "They're going to keep a police officer here to watch over our house to make sure nothing more happens."

Ben seemed to accept that at face value. She'd expected dozens of questions, but he surprised her by changing the subject. "Are we still going swimming?"

"Absolutely." Joel slid behind the wheel. The SUV engine had been idling the whole time to keep Ben and Royal cool, so he put the car in gear and pulled away from the curb. "We'll have a great time."

As Joel drove down the street, Trina watched via the side mirror as the firefighters conversed with the

Cody police officers. She hoped their canvass of the neighborhood and checking gas station video in town would give them something to work with.

The sooner the Cody police arrested the arsonist, the better.

THE PUNGENT SCENT of gasoline and smoke clung to Joel's hands and clothes. He kept a keen eye on the rearview mirror to make sure they weren't followed. And to be extra safe, he made several turns, going around blocks and eventually approaching the Elk Lodge from the opposite direction.

He'd tried not to show Trina how concerned he was about the escalation to arson. Not that firing a gun at someone was any better than starting a fire. Yet if the intent was to kill them, why not wait until the middle of the night to start the fire? Sure, flames were easier seen in the dark, but choosing to strike at night had a higher chance of success.

He didn't understand what the arsonist's motive was here. To instill panic and fear? Or to kill Trina —why? To get custody of Ben?

Either way, he'd already decided to call both Doug and Griff as soon as they arrived back at the hotel. Considering the escalation tactic of turning to arson, he'd feel better having additional resources working with the local police.

He pulled around to the back of the hotel, so that his SUV wasn't in plain view of the main thoroughfare. He released the back hatch for Royal, as Trina waited for Ben to climb out.

Moments later, they were back in the hotel room. The gasoline scent clung to his clothing and skin, so he gestured toward the second bedroom. "Sorry to make you wait, but I need to take a shower."

"Go ahead." Trina turned to Ben. "You have time to play with Royal while we wait."

Ben ran around, inviting Royal to chase him. Royal looked torn as to whom to follow but eventually trotted after Ben. Maybe his K9 didn't like the smell of gasoline, or maybe Royal understood Ben and Trina were in danger.

In the bathroom, Joel stuffed his stinky clothes into a plastic bag, then stood in the shower, scrubbing every inch of his skin with soap. Finally, he climbed out, dried off, and donned clean clothes. The gasoline scent lingered, so he knotted the plastic bag holding his clothes tightly. He was half tempted to toss them, but he wasn't sure if he'd need to wear them again at some point.

"Hurry, Joel." Ben jumped from one foot to the other as if he couldn't stand still. Trina was wearing shorts, a T-shirt, and flip-flops. No doubt in case she had to get into the water with Ben. "I wanna swim with Royal!"

"I'm ready, but I don't know that they'll allow Royal in the pool." He belatedly realized he shouldn't have brought up the subject of how labs like to swim. Kids had a way of remembering details you'd rather they forget. "The pool might only be for kids and parents, not dogs."

"They will." Ben shrugged off that as unimportant.

"Don't forget a towel," Trina called as Ben ran toward the door.

The boy glanced at her, sighed, then returned to the sofa to grab the folded towel. Joel, Trina, and Royal followed Ben down the hall to the indoor pool. A glance through the window confirmed the pool area was empty. He was surprised, considering it was summer and this was when tourists flocked to the area. Maybe because today was Wednesday, smack dab in the middle of the week.

The chlorine scent was strong enough to eliminate the last bit of gasoline that seemed to be seared into his nasal passages.

"Slowly, Ben," Trina called as the boy raced toward the pool. "Don't slip and fall."

"I won't," Ben assured her.

"Trina, I have some calls to make." He stopped at

a large patio table in one corner of the room. "I want to follow up with my family."

"Okay." She hurried toward Ben who was already going down the concrete steps of the shallow end of the pool. "Be careful, Ben. Do you know how to swim?"

"Yes." The way Ben clung to the side of the pool made Joel think the kid was overestimating his ability.

"Stay in the shallow end." Trina's voice was firm. "I don't have a swimming suit to jump into the water to rescue you."

"Okay." Ben splashed Royal, grinning when the dog shook his body to get rid of the excess water. "Wanna swim, Royal?"

Joel crossed over to prevent the dog from going in. When Royal stretched out on the concrete to watch. rather than jumping into the water to play with Ben, he bent over to stroke the dog's silky fur. "Good boy," he murmured. "Watch him, okay?"

Royal thumped his tail, his gaze seemingly fixated on Ben.

Joel moved back toward the table. Scrolling through his contact list, he settled on Griff. Better to start with the FBI rather than Doug with the DEA. This wasn't about drugs from what he could tell.

Granted, shooting and arson didn't exactly fall into Griff's jurisdiction either. But he wasn't above playing the future brother-in-law card. Not when a woman and her child were in danger.

"Joel? Something wrong?" Griff's tone held concern.

"Yeah, Griff, I have a situation," Joel admitted. He went on to fill his sister's fiancé about the shooting attempts and the arson. "The Cody police are working the case, but I'm not sure how familiar they are with incidents involving arson. And I'm concerned our suspect is from outside the city, like the Laramie area, which might hamper their investigation."

"Give me the names of all possible suspects," Griff said without hesitation. "I'll run them through our database to see what pops. And I can call Laramie as well. Maybe I can encourage them to cooperate. I'm sure they'd rather work with the Cody PD than risk the feds taking over their case."

"Thanks." He took a moment to provide the details of the two men in Evie's life along with Trina's previous boyfriends.

"Do you really think one of Trina's boyfriends are involved?" Griff asked, doubt in his voice.

"Probably not, but I wanted to cover all bases." He flushed, wondering if it was his own dating experience that had colored his attitude. "If you ask me, it's strange that these incidents happened within weeks of Trina moving Ben to her place in Cody. If

Ben's father, Brian Ashland, wanted custody of his son, why not act while she was in Laramie? Why wait until she was settled here in Cody?"

"Maybe he thought that would be too obvious? That waiting to strike out at Trina in Cody would cover his tracks so nobody would suspect him?" Griff sighed loudly. "Anyone in law enforcement always puts the spouse or ex-spouse at the top of a suspect list. No matter where they live."

"Yeah, that makes sense." Joel raked his hand through his hair. "I'm trying to understand the logic."

Griff barked out a laugh. "Are you kidding me? Most of these perps think they're invincible. They tend to believe they're smarter than they really are. And logic is rarely front and center in their thought process.

"Yeah, I guess." Ben was dog-paddling across the width of the pool. Maybe the kid had taken some swimming lessons. Trina watched him like a hawk, as did Royal. Reassured, he turned his attention back to Griff. "I was planning to call Doug too. See what he thinks about all of this."

"I'm working from the ranch today, I'll fill him in when I see him," Griff offered. The FBI offices were in Cheyenne, but since getting engaged and soon to be married to Joel's sister Alexis, Griff had gotten permission to work from the ranch a few days every week. The fact that the ranch was more centrally located, compared to Cheyenne, had worked to Griff's advantage. "Do you want us to head out to meet up with you and Trina in Cody?"

"No thanks." As much as he wanted help in finding this guy, Joel didn't want to be a burden. "I think we're safe here. I made sure we weren't followed. The fact that the fire was started after we headed into town to check into the hotel tells me the guy probably didn't realize we had left the property in the first place."

"Okay, but if that changes, let me know," Griff said. "I'm not too busy that I can't make this a priority."

"I will." He was glad to have Griff's support. "Let me know if you come up with anything."

"Understood. Hey, looks like my boss is calling, so I better take this. I'll be in touch." With that, Griff ended the call.

Joel set his phone on the table. Talking to Griff helped, but he still felt on edge. Like there was more he should be doing to get to the bottom of this mess. He'd never worked law enforcement the way his older sister Maya had or his sister Jessica who'd worked TSA at the Cheyenne airport. His experience was limited to search and rescue.

And while he and his Sullivan siblings had certainly uncovered and helped solve many crimes over the past few months, they'd done so with the help of law enforcement. He hoped and prayed Griff would come through for them.

Trina stood on the concrete steps of the pool, the water lapping over her knees. Her smile was strained, but he doubted Ben picked up on her stress. Not that kids couldn't be perceptive. He knew they often absorbed more than their parents gave them credit for. But in this case, Ben splashed and played in the water, clearly enjoying himself.

Joel briefly wondered if these attacks could in any way be related to his family, then dismissed the idea. There was no reason to set fire to Trina's house if someone was mad at him or one of his siblings. It would make more sense for the ranch to be targeted.

No, this had to be related to Trina and Ben. How, he wasn't sure.

He crossed over to where Trina stood in the shallow end of the pool. "I can watch Ben if you'd like to call your insurance company."

She hesitated, appearing uncertain whether she should delegate the responsibility for Ben to someone else.

"We all chip in to help my brother Chase and his wife, Wynona, with their five-year-old son, Eli," he said. "Don't feel as if you have to do everything alone."

She grimaced. "Easy to say, not as easy to do. I

am Ben's sole guardian. To be honest, I have a new respect for what my sister went through after her divorce. Being a single parent isn't easy."

"Especially not for you, Trina. You've had to pick up where your sister left off, without any preparation at all." He held out his hand. "Take a break. Royal and I are here to watch over Ben."

That made her smile. She placed her hand in his and leaned on him to step back out of the pool.

The fleeting touch sent a weird awareness zinging through his blood stream. Not cool. He turned his attention to the pool, reminding himself that his only reason for being there was to keep Trina and Ben safe.

A relationship was out of the question.

He turned to look through the glass window lining the wall behind him. The hallway beyond appeared empty. He still found it strange that they were the only ones here enjoying the facility.

A sudden harsh coughing had him spinning back to the pool. Ben's face was red as he struggled to breathe, his arms flailing in the water.

Royal jumped up and leaped into the water, paddling toward Ben. Joel kicked off his shoes and stripped off his shirt before jumping in after his K9. He reached Ben in seconds, scooping the boy up and out of the water to hold him against his chest.

"Easy now, you're safe. Try to breathe. Can you talk?"

Ben shook his head, coughing frantically against the water he'd obviously inhaled by accident.

"You're safe," Joel repeated as he strode through the pool toward the steps. The fact that Ben was taking a few gasping breaths meant he didn't have to perform rescue breathing. Joel took the steps up to the edge, his jeans plastered to his legs, huge water puddles forming around his bare feet.

Trina hurried over, her expression full of concern. "What happened?"

He kicked himself for taking his eyes off Ben even for a second. "I'm sorry. I should have watched him more closely. I think he accidentally went under and inhaled some water for his efforts."

"Ben? Are you okay?" She ran her hand down Ben's back.

The little boy's coughing finally eased, and the boy began to breathe easier. Ben rested his head against Joel's chest. After a few moments, the little boy said, "I swallowed some water."

"I know." He glanced over to where Royal had gotten out of the pool. The dog came over to sniff at his feet, then shook himself to get rid of the excess water, drenching Trina. Joel was already soaking wet. "I'm sorry that happened. Did you see how Royal jumped into the water to rescue you?"

Ben nodded, his head still on his chest. "You were right. He knows how to swim."

"Did you really take swimming lessons, Ben?" Trina wiped water from her face.

"Sort of." Ben pressed his face farther into Joel's chest. "One class. Then Mom said I couldn't go anymore."

Trina frowned, catching Joel's gaze. Clearly that one class thing was news to her. And why had her sister stopped the classes?

He slid his arm around her to reassure them both that everything was fine.

But deep down, he felt responsible for the near-drowning incident. He needed to do better or risk failing in his promise to keep them safe.

5

———————

Joel's warm embrace made Trina wish for something she couldn't have. Ben was already becoming too attached to Joel.

The same way she was.

Drawing a deep breath, she reluctantly eased away. Joel was only there to protect them. Nothing more. Thankfully, Ben was safe. And as she feared, his swimming skills were limited to the dog paddle.

Why on earth had Evie enrolled Ben in swimming lessons, then stopped them? Had that been around the time of her divorce? That made the most sense, although she made a mental note to ask Ben more about his life with her sister prior to her accident. Maybe there was more to Evie and Brian's split than her sister had let on.

"I'll need to change." Joel bent to put Ben down, eyeing his sopping-wet jeans with a grimace. "I think I have a pair of shorts in my duffel. My other clothing reeks of smoke and gasoline."

"I'm sure they have a laundry here." She felt guilty over his needing to jump in to save her nephew. "I can do a quick load for you."

He waved a hand. "I'm capable of doing that myself."

She grabbed the towel Ben had brought from their room and wrapped it around his shoulders.

"Royal needs a towel too." Ben looked up at her. "He jumped in to save me."

"I know. He's an amazing dog, isn't he?" She pulled Ben in for a quick hug. "We'll grab another towel for Royal back in our room."

"Can we swim again later?" Ben shrugged off the towel and ran ahead to open the door.

She was surprised Ben wanted to go back into the water. She glanced questioningly at Joel, who nodded in agreement. "Sure. But for now, we'll see what there is to watch on television."

"Okay." Ben was still young enough to watch shows on the kids' channel. She supposed that would change in a few years. Hard to believe he would start third grade in a few weeks. She felt woefully unprepared for raising Ben. Not that she had a choice.

When the adoption went through, she'd legally be Ben's mother. Not that she expected he'd call her mom. She didn't want to replace Evie in the boy's life. Losing his father to divorce, then his mother to death was more than enough for any child to deal with.

She'd accept her role as Ben's aunt.

Joel padded down the hallway in his bare feet, carrying his shirt, shoes, and phone in one hand. His wallet had been soaked, too, but he didn't complain. Joel was being remarkably nice about everything.

Especially since she was the one in danger.

He'd taken over the role of their protector without asking for anything in return. She admired him more than she could say. For being there now and dedicating his life to search and rescue missions.

But admiring him from afar was all she could do. She needed to protect her foolish heart.

Once they were back in the suite, she grabbed another towel to use on Royal. The dog let her swipe the towel over him but then shook himself again. She tossed the towel aside, deciding to let him dry naturally.

Joel disappeared into his room, emerging a few minutes later wearing cargo shorts and a T-shirt, his wet jeans stuffed in a plastic bag. He was so handsome she had to force herself to look away.

"Stay, Royal," Joel commanded. The dog obediently stretched out on the floor. "Good boy. Wait here for me, Trina, and don't open the door for anyone. I have my key." He reached for the door handle. "I'll be back in a few minutes."

"Okay." After he left the room, she turned toward Ben. "Where's the remote control for the TV?"

"Here." He held it up, then expertly turned it on and began flipping through channels.

Leaving him to it, she dropped into the closest chair feeling suddenly exhausted. The emotional turmoil of the gunfire, arson, and Ben's choking incident hit her like a brick. She scrubbed her hands over her face, then had to smile when Royal stood, crossed to the door, and then lay back down again. The K9 positioned himself so that his back was to the doorway, facing her and Ben.

Their protector, she thought with a wry smile. The black lab was truly amazing.

She wanted to quiz Ben on how things were between his mother and Peter Thomas, but his attention was riveted on the television. She didn't like the idea of reminding him of his loss, but they needed something to go on.

Sooner rather than later.

A few minutes later, Joel returned. The minute

he used his key card to electronically unlock the door, Royal jumped up and backed away, his tail wagging back and forth.

"All set. Good boy, Royal." Joel bent to pet the dog, then opened his wallet to spread everything out on the table to dry. He arched a brow when he found Ben glued to the television. "Let me know when you and Ben are hungry for lunch. They have a decent room service menu." He hesitated, then added, "I'd rather not go to the Hitching Post, even though it's right across the street."

She nodded, feeling safer here in the hotel room than outside. She rose to join him at the table. "How long will it take you to hear back from your brother-in-law?"

"Not sure." He frowned. "It's possible none of these guys has a criminal background. And if that's the case, their fingerprints or DNA are likely not in the system."

She glanced at Ben. "I'd like to ask him some questions about his mother and her relationship with Peter Thomas, but I'm afraid of upsetting him."

Joel lightly touched her arm. "You'll have to take the risk, Trina."

"Okay." She steeled her resolve. "The show he's watching is more than half over, so when that's finished, we'll talk over lunch."

"Good plan." Joel leaned forward and snagged

the room service menu. "Choose something you and Ben would like. Room service can take up to an hour to be delivered."

The menu wasn't extensive, but there were two items she knew Ben would like. Yet she also knew from experience it was best to ask him. She took the menu to the sofa. "Ben, do you want chicken tenders with fries or a hot dog?"

"Tenders with fries," he said without looking at her.

She ran her hand over his now mostly dry hair. "Sounds good."

Joel used the hotel phone to place their order. After a half hour or so, he glanced at his watch and stood. "I need to check the laundry."

Hearing the end of the movie on the television made her stand. "Turn it off now, Ben." She gestured to the remote. "Lunch will be here soon."

"Okay." He did as she asked, then sat down on the floor beside Royal. "Aunt Trina, you won't forget about our puppy, right?"

"I won't forget." She smiled. "We'll ask Joel for help in picking one out."

Ben nodded, stroking his hand over Royal's now dry fur. "I want my puppy to be just like Royal."

"Every dog has their own personality," she said. "Just like people do."

Ben frowned at that, then shrugged. "We'll get a black dog just like Royal."

She swallowed a sigh. What were the chances they'd find a black lab like Royal? Not good. Joel returned to the room five minutes before their lunch arrived.

When they were seated at the table, Joel glanced at her. "I'd like to say grace."

"Of course." She should have anticipated that after their breakfast. "Fold your hands together like this, Ben." She showed him how.

"Dear Lord Jesus, we thank You for this food and for keeping us safe in Your care. Please guide the police so they may find and arrest the person responsible. Amen."

"Amen," she echoed.

Ben took a french fry. "Yum."

She smiled, then remembering her promise to Joel, asked, "Ben, did you meet your mom's boyfriend, Peter?"

Ben nodded. "Yep."

"Did you like him?" She held the boy's gaze, trying to assess whether the question upset him. "Was he nice to you?"

"Sort of." Ben shrugged and picked up another fry. "I liked him better when he and Mom didn't yell at each other."

Yelling? She glanced at Joel for a moment, then asked, "What did they argue about?"

Another shrug. "Stuff. I always had to go to my room when they were fighting."

That did not sound good. Evie hadn't mentioned having issues with her boyfriend. Then again, Evie hadn't said much about Peter at all. At the time, Trina had assumed they weren't very serious. Now she wasn't so sure. "Did they yell a lot?"

Ben scrunched up his face. "Not every day. Sometimes Mom would tell him to go home because she didn't want to talk to him anymore."

Now that sounded like Evie. Trina was secretly glad to know Peter hadn't lived with Evie and Ben. At least her sister had kept her independence. A tough lesson Evie had learned the hard way after her divorce.

"I remember Mom told Peter he had to pay her back," Ben said suddenly. "By the end of the month."

Pay her back? She glanced at Joel who was listening to their conversation with keen interest. Had Evie loaned Peter money? If so, why?

"Do you know if Peter paid her back?" she asked, trying to sound nonchalant.

"I dunno." Ben dipped a chicken tender into a blob of ketchup.

She took a bite of her turkey club, then pulled

out her phone, scrolling to look at the calendar. Evie's biking accident had been on May 24, and she'd passed away two days later on the 26th.

She frowned, thinking back to those chaotic days and weeks after Evie's passing. Ben had been at school that day. When the hospital called to let Trina know, she'd rushed to Laramie to pick Ben up. They'd gone together to visit Evie. Her sister had been badly injured, several broken bones including her back, her pelvis, and her legs. But it had been Evie's head injury that had concerned the medical team the most.

The doctor and nurses had been kind and supportive, but Trina had known from the beginning they'd expected Evie to die. That her wounds were simply too severe for her sister to recover.

Trina had stayed with Ben in Evie's apartment. After Evie's death, she'd had to wait for the official death certificate to access Evie's accounts. Trina had paid the rent out of her own pocket because it had taken a full two weeks to get access to Evie's money. She'd been surprised that her sister only had a thousand dollars in her checking account and two hundred in her savings. That had been just enough to cover her June rent, without much leftover to buy groceries, gas, and other necessities. Trina had wondered why her sister was living paycheck to paycheck since Evie had a good job as an administrative assistant for the CEO of a company. Trina had learned her sister had been given a few days off because the CEO was out of town.

Vacation days that had tragically resulted in Evie's death.

At the time, the police had claimed Evie had been alone when she'd crashed into that tree going at a high rate of speed down a steep hill. There had even been a hint of possible suicide, but Trina had assured them her sister would never do such a thing. She was convinced it was nothing more than a terrible accident.

Her stomach tightened. What if she and the police were wrong? What if Evie crashing her bike wasn't an accident at all? What if Peter had gotten upset enough to cause the collision? Could he have tampered with her brakes to avoid having to pay Evie back the money he'd borrowed?

She knew she was letting her thoughts go wild, but she couldn't seem to stop. Especially now that she knew Evie and Peter had argued a lot and that there was a financial dispute.

Yet even if Peter had decided to take drastic action that day, it didn't make sense that the guy would come after her and Ben now. Not when he'd already gotten away with not having to pay back any of the money Evie had loaned him.

On the heels of that came a darker thought.

Maybe Peter needed more money and had come to Cody to figure out a way to use Ben as leverage to get it.

~

Joel had kept quiet as Trina had carefully questioned Ben about his mother's relationship with Peter Thomas. Trina's thoughts were plainly etched on her face, and the moment they'd finished eating and Ben returned to his television show with Royal following him to the sofa, she leaned toward him.

"We need to talk to the Laramie police." Her voice was low enough that Ben couldn't overhear.

"Griff, my future brother-in-law, is going to do that." He smiled at how Ben snuggled up with Royal. "And so are the Cody police officers."

"I know, but this is new information." Trina's brown eyes were full of anguish. "I didn't know Evie's relationship with Peter included arguing over money. It never occurred to me that Evie may have been killed."

"Whoa, Trina, you don't know that." He understood her concern, but that was a leap. "Arguing and borrowing money doesn't equate to murder."

"But it is something none of us knew prior to this. And you know as well as I do that some people will do anything for money." She set her jaw stubbornly. "I'm telling you, the Laramie police need to question Peter Thomas right away."

"Okay, I'll follow up with Griff and the local cops." He reached over to take her hand. "But seriously, try not to let your imagination run wild."

Trina narrowed her gaze, tugging free of his grip. "I didn't imagine two incidents of gunfire or my house being set on fire."

He winced. "Of course not. Let's just try to keep an open mind, okay?"

"Fine." She still looked annoyed. "I don't care what you say, Joel, in my mind Peter is now a prime suspect."

He decided that arguing was fruitless and gestured to her phone. "Do you think you can find Peter on social media? Maybe we'll learn something from his posts."

She brightened at the suggestion. "I'll do my best. I mostly use social media for my books, not for posting about my personal life. I don't want people to know who I am or where I live."

"Ditto," he agreed. "The ranch has a social media presence, but we're vague when it comes to members of the family. Kendra does most of the work, and she keeps our posts focused on the dogs."

"Smarter that way." She wrinkled her nose as

she opened an app on her phone. "I use a pseudonym to protect my privacy."

"Oh yeah?" He leaned forward to see her screen. "What name to you use?"

"Doesn't matter." She moved the phone away so he couldn't see, flashing a teasing smile. "I don't write books you'd have any interest in reading, remember?"

"Hey, I have sisters." He was happy she wasn't still upset with him. "Besides, I like a good mystery."

She ignored that, scrolling intently through her phone. Leaving her to it, he cleaned up the mess from their meal and set the tray outside in the hallway. Wandering over to the sofa, he leaned over to smooth a hand over Royal's fur, eyeing the television curiously. "What are you watching?"

Ben didn't look at him. "LEGO City."

He'd never heard of it. It might have been something his nephew Eli watched, but he wouldn't know. He and Justin were teaching the little boy to ride a horse. Eli was quiet around people, having to be reminded to use his words when he wanted something. Around animals, the little boy blossomed. Eli loved riding and playing with the dogs.

Glancing at his watch, Joel realized it was time to get his clothes from the dryer. When he headed to the door, his K9 lifted his head as if to follow. "No, Royal. Stay."

Royal watched as he pocketed his key and left the room. The dryer was finished. He sniffed his clothes, glad the gasoline and smoke scent were gone. After returning to the room, he quickly changed back into his jeans. He put the mostly dry cash back into his wallet and tucked that away too.

The long afternoon stretched before him. Joel wasn't accustomed to sitting around in a hotel room. He checked his phone but had not gotten any updates from Griff or the Cody police.

"I found Peter Thomas," Trina said. "But it's weird that he hasn't posted anything since Evie's passing."

He moved over to sit beside her. "Maybe he's upset over her death."

"Or he's responsible for it," she shot back.

He swallowed a sigh. She was like a dog with a bone. "I'll call Griff. See if he's found anything."

"Thank you."

His future brother-in-law answered on the first ring. "Everything okay?" Griff asked.

"Fine. Just some new information." He filled Griff in the arguing and possible financial angle.

"I've spoken with the Laramie PD," Griff said. "They gave no indication Evie's death was anything but a tragic accident."

"I know, but shouldn't they at least chat with Thomas?" Trina scowled, obviously listening to his side of the conversation. "It wouldn't hurt to cover their bases."

"I'll suggest that," Griff agreed. "But I didn't find anything criminal in his background check or any of the other names you gave me. The ex-husband, Brian Ashland? He has some minor credit card debt. Nothing too crazy."

"No criminal background issues and just Ashland has credit card debt?" He repeated the information for Trina. "Okay, that helps. I found a shell casing at the scene but haven't heard if prints were found. I plan to call the Cody PD next."

"Do that and let me know if you need anything else," Griff said. "The more I realize how little intel we have, the more I think we should have the Laramie PD interview both Brian Ashland and Peter Thomas. If nothing else, I'd like them to verify that both men are still in Laramie."

"Thanks, Griff." He ended the call, then scrolled through his contacts to find the number for Burt Jones. Over the past few years, he and his siblings had gotten to know the Cody police on a first-name basis. The local law enforcement agencies were quick to call on the Sullivan K9 handlers for help with missing persons and sometimes for criminals on the run.

"Hey, Joel, sorry I didn't get back to you sooner," Burt said. "None of Trina's neighbors saw anything useful. We started looking at gas station video but haven't noticed anyone suspicious filling a portable gas can prior to the arson attempt. Granted we've only checked a couple of them so far."

"Thanks for letting me know. But what about the shell casing I found? Any prints from that?"

"We did get a partial print, but there was no match in the system." Burt sounded tired. "Unfortunately, we're running out of leads."

"Do me a favor and pull driver's license photos for Brian Ashland and Peter Thomas," Joel said. "They were in a relationship with Evie, Trina's sister and Ben's mother, and they both have some cash flow issues. Maybe someone will recognize them."

"I did that with Ashland's photo, but I can go back with the other one." Burt sounded interested in having another angle to work. "Can't hurt."

"Thank you." He didn't mention his conversation with Griff. "Let me know if you learn anything."

"Will do." Burt ended the call.

"Nothing yet?" Trina looked frustrated. "It's hard to believe nobody saw anything." Then she flushed and added, "Not that I'm the most observant neighbor either. I guess I need to do better too."

He shrugged. "Don't beat yourself up. Cody isn't exactly a high crime area. The locals don't pay that much attention to strangers walking around, especially in the height of tourist season. Burt agreed to flash Peter's photo around. Maybe that will help."

"I hope so." She glanced over to where Royal was sleeping beside Ben. "Maybe I should get my laptop from the car. Sitting around like this will drive me crazy. I should try to get some writing done."

He nodded and rose to his feet. "I'll grab it for you."

"Joel? Can I get my video game now?" Ben's voice from the sofa drew his attention. "My show's over."

"Ah, not right now, but later, okay?" He didn't want Ben or Trina anywhere near their house when the police were no closer to finding the arsonist.

Ben's disappointed expression hit hard. He was tempted to offer to buy a replacement but sensed Trina wouldn't approve.

He had barely taken two steps toward the door when a blaring sound pierced the room. It took a moment for Joel to realize it was a fire alarm.

Two fires in one day? A coincidence? He didn't believe it, but he didn't want to sound paranoid either.

"What's that noise!" Ben covered his ears with his hands as Royal jumped off the sofa, ears perked up. "Make it stop!"

Trina hurried over. "We need to go."

"Yeah, I know." Joel didn't like it but reached for the door. "Stay close, okay?"

Trina's brown eyes widened as she realized he was concerned about their safety. "Come, Ben."

Still covering his ears, Ben crossed over to stand beside Trina. Joel led the way, with Royal at his heels. Trina hovered close, keeping a protective arm around Ben. As they made their way down the hallway to the closest exit, he frowned when he didn't detect a hint of smoke. Logically, he knew it could be that some room on the opposite side of the building was the source of the blaze.

Or it could be a prank.

Worst-case scenario was that someone had pulled the alarm deliberately to flush them out of the room.

Joel pushed through the door first, squinting against the bright sunlight. Royal lifted his snout to the breeze, sniffing with interest.

Trina and Ben crowded close. "Where do we go?" Trina asked.

"The SUV." He scanned the area but didn't see anything alarming. More people were coming out of the hotel now, so he moved quickly toward his vehicle.

The urge to get far away was difficult to ignore.

He was within ten feet of the SUV when he heard the crack of gunfire seconds before the windshield shattered. Stopping abruptly, he jutted to the side, turned, and scooped Ben into his arms. "To the trees," he shouted.

Trina didn't hesitate to run toward shelter. Royal ran alongside them. Joel hunched his shoulders, expecting to be shot in the back at any moment.

Praying with his whole heart that he'd find a way to keep Trina and Ben safe.

6

———————

A trap! Trina's heart thundered in her chest as she darted toward the scraggly trees along the back of the parking lot. She couldn't believe the fire alarm had been pulled just to get them out of the hotel. Yet that's exactly what had happened.

The trees weren't thick enough for her peace of mind. She huddled near Joel and Royal, humbled by how Joel had instantly carried Ben to safety. The gunfire on the heels of the fire alarm caused chaos. People screamed and scattered, taking off in different directions. The confusion helped a little, but she still felt vulnerable.

They had to assume the killer was hunkered down nearby, waiting for another opportunity to fire at them.

At her. She'd been the person closest to the SUV.

"We need to get out of here," Joel said in a low whisper. He had his arm clamped around Ben, keeping him close. To his credit, Ben wasn't crying, but his brown eyes were wide with fear as he gripped Royal's collar. Her nephew was likely in shock. She didn't blame him; she felt as if she'd been dropped in the middle of a horror flick too.

"Go where?" She knew the vehicle wasn't an option. "Two adults, one kid, and a dog will be noticeable. What if the gunman sees us?"

"I don't like it either," Joel muttered. He shifted to pull out his phone.

The shrill sound of wailing sirens filled the air. She realized that whoever had pulled the fire alarm hadn't anticipated the fire department would be instantly notified as well.

The police would arrive soon too.

Long seconds passed without incident. The hotel parking lot was pretty much emptied out now. She couldn't help but wonder who was out there. Brian Ashland? Peter Thomas?

Someone else?

"Let's hold our position for a few minutes." Joel raised his voice to be heard above the sirens.

Another crack of gunfire rang out. Trina gasped

when a piece of bark flew off the tree beside her, mere inches from her face.

"Down!" Joel's large hand shoved hard on her head.

Ben burst into tears now, sobbing with fear. "Auntie Trina!"

"I'm fine, Ben." She drew him close, sandwiching him between her, Joel and Royal. "We're okay. The police will be here any minute."

Brave words, but her heart thundered in her chest as she realized the killer had gotten far too close. And worse, she grimly realized that Peter or Brian or whoever was out there was intent on killing her. But why?

To get custody of Ben? Or for some other nefarious reason?

Heaven help her, she didn't know!

As if on cue, the same firetruck that had responded to the fire at her home pulled into the parking lot. She tried to lift her head to see better, but Joel still held her down. When she caught a glimpse of a police car arriving on the scene, he finally eased up.

"Wait for the police to come to us." Joel stroked Royal's fur. The dog didn't bark or growl, but his nose quivered as he took in the various scents.

She frowned, wondering how they'd even know

they were hiding there. But they must not have been as hidden as she'd believed because Heath Anderson rushed toward them.

"Anyone hurt?" He scowled, raking his gaze over them.

"I don't think so." She took a moment to examine Ben more closely. His sobs had dwindled with the arrival of the police and firefighters. She was reassured that they hadn't been physically wounded.

But emotionally she knew Ben couldn't take much more. Terrified didn't begin to cover it. A flash of anger hit hard. She wanted the person responsible for putting them through this found and arrested!

"What happened?" Heath asked, his brow furrowed with concern. "We got the notice of the fire alarm, then reports of gunfire poured in."

"The fire alarm was to force us out of the building." Joel narrowed his eyes. "I had a feeling it was a false alarm, but it wasn't until a bullet shattered my windshield that my suspicions were confirmed."

Burt Jones jogged over to join them. "Did you see who did this?"

"No, I'm afraid not." Trina forced herself to be calm for Ben's sake. "I mean, there were plenty of people streaming out of the hotel and scattering when gunfire rang out. But I didn't see anyone acting suspicious."

"I didn't either," Joel said. He glanced down at Royal, then at her and Ben. "We're blessed to have escaped unharmed."

She couldn't disagree. Maybe God was watching over them. She managed to nod. "Very much so."

"We need a ride," Joel said. "I'll call my siblings for help, but it will take time for them to get here."

"Of course." Heath didn't hesitate. "Give us a few minutes to clear the area."

She swallowed her protest. Better for the police to make sure the gunman wasn't hiding nearby.

Brian? Peter? Someone else? Her thoughts whirled, the names circling her brain like a tape stuck in a loop. Brian? Peter? Someone else?

"Aunt Trina, where are we going now?" Ben's expression betrayed his concern. "I thought we were safe here."

"You're always safe with me and Joel. Royal too," she added.

"I love Royal." When Ben stroked the dog's fur, Royal licked his cheek. Ben buried his face against the dog's fur. And she wished more than anything she could make this easier for the little boy.

It took a moment to realize Joel was on his phone. Shoving thoughts of the gunman away, she listened to his side of the conversation. "Yeah, a spare SUV and extra cash. Thanks, Justin. See you and Trevor soon." He pocketed the phone. "We'll get a ride from the police and then figure out our next steps."

"I'm glad." No surprise his siblings had dropped everything to respond to Joel's cry for help. She and Evie had been close, too, at one point. Less so in recent years and Trina wished now she'd had made the trip to Laramie more often.

She closed her eyes on a wave of despair. Regret burned hot in the back of her throat.

"Don't, Trina. It's going to work out," Joel said in a low, comforting tone. "We'll get through this."

She managed a weak nod. Shoving the emotion aside, she focused on Ben. Her nephew, soon to be her adopted son, was all that mattered.

"Joel? Are you guys ready to go?"

"Yeah." Joel stood. He waited for her and Ben to get up from the ground too. "Come, Royal."

The black lab abruptly darted forward. Keeping his nose to the ground, Royal headed to the far corner of the building.

"Is Royal running away?" Ben asked fearfully as Joel sprinted after his K9.

"I don't think so." She knew Royal was too well trained for that. Her pulse spiked at the possibility Royal had caught the scent of the gunman. "Look, see how Royal has his nose to the ground, moving from side to side? I believe he's searching for something."

Heath crossed over to her and Ben. "What's up with Royal?"

She shrugged. "He could be searching for another shell casing."

Heath nodded. "That would be helpful. As soon as they return, we'll head out. My squad is the closest one."

She nodded but didn't move toward the car. It would be too hot to sit inside to wait. And she wanted to understand what Royal had found.

Thankfully, it didn't take too long. Joel had a satisfied expression on his face when they returned. He held up a small plastic bag containing a shell casing. "Heath, I need you to get this to the lab, see if it's a match to the one Royal found earlier this morning."

"I'm surprised the dog searched for it without being told." Heath took the evidence. "He's pretty smart."

"Very smart," Joel agreed. "I believe he caught the gunman's scent. Finding the shell casing was secondary."

"He can do that?" Trina looked down at Royal in surprise. "I thought he needed a scent source, like clothing?"

"Typically, yes, but our K9s are on alert for danger." Joel dropped to a knee to run his fingers over

Royal's fur. "You're a good boy, aren't you?" He grimaced. "I didn't have my backpack to reward him properly with his stuffed beaver."

"My laptop is in the room too," she said. "And I would rather not leave it behind."

"I'll grab your things," Heath offered. "Stay here, I'll be back soon."

There were plenty of people milling about now, mostly law enforcement and firefighters. It was clear the hotel had not been on fire. "Joel?" She moved closer to him. "Would the hotel have security cameras?"

He nodded. "They have one camera overlooking the front of the building." He gestured to where Burt Jones was speaking with a middle-aged bald man. "I believe that's what Burt is asking about now."

"They'll know if Brian or Peter show up on the video." As soon as the words left her mouth, she knew that didn't mean much. "Although I'm sure someone could get inside by simply waiting by the side exit for someone to head out."

"Yep." Joel grimaced. "I wouldn't hold my breath that they'll find anything useful on the security camera."

She swallowed against a lump of frustration. Whoever was orchestrating this nightmare seemed to be one step ahead of them every single time.

And she was growing increasingly worried they wouldn't figure out who was responsible in time to prevent another deadly attack.

~

JOEL TRIED to be patient as they waited for Heath to bring their stuff out of the hotel room. It wasn't that he didn't trust the local cops, but he had more faith in his family. And the sooner his brothers arrived in Cody, the better.

Justin had agreed to update Griff prior to heading out. He and Trevor would drive separate vehicles, leaving one for Joel and Trina to use.

He noticed Royal seemed to stay near Ben, as if the K9 knew his job was to protect the boy from harm. Labs weren't known to be attack dogs, but Royal would certainly growl and bark if anyone got too close.

Especially the gunman. Joel was convinced Royal had the killer's scent stored in his memory.

Despite his efforts to avoid being followed, Joel had to assume the gunman had figured out what car they were using. Since he hadn't known which room they were in, he pulled the fire alarm to flush them out. Striking his SUV with a bullet had not been an accident.

Message received, he thought with a dark scowl. Three shooting incidents and a fire all in one day.

Worse, it was early afternoon. The escalating attempts reminded him of the serial killer who'd become obsessed with his sister Alexis a few weeks ago.

"I think I have everything." Heath strode toward them, pulling the rolling suitcase with Joel's backpack over one shoulder and Trina's computer bag on the other.

"Thanks." Joel reached for the pack. He took a moment to give Royal some water. The dog lapped eagerly, then looked up at Joel as if expecting to be put to work. "Not yet, boy." He stroked the lab's fur. "Soon."

Royal wagged his tail as if in understanding. A few minutes later, they were on the road heading away from the Elk Lodge.

"Where to?" Heath asked.

It was a good question. Joel turned to glance at Trina and Ben who were seated in the back with Royal on the floor at Ben's feet.

"Not the Wild Bill," Trina said. "That place is awful."

"I wasn't planning to head there," he agreed. "What about the Frontier?"

"Okay." She frowned. "I hate wasting money, though. We paid for a suite we can't even use."

He waved that off. "Take us to the Frontier," he told Heath. "We may not stay there for long, but it'll work for the interim."

Heath frowned. "Where will you go?"

"I'm not sure." In truth, Joel didn't like his options. A hotel might be too obvious, and there were only so many places in town. If the gunman really wanted to find them, he could probably use the process of elimination.

Yet using the ranch was out of the question. No way would he put two pregnant women and his nephew at risk.

A rental could work, as long as it was a place that wasn't too obvious. Maybe outside of the Cody city limits? He'd prefer an isolated cabin somewhere in the middle of the woods.

"I have'ta go to the bathroom," Ben announced.

"Okay, we're almost at the hotel." He turned to look at Ben. "Can you wait that long?"

Ben nodded, but from the expression on his face, Joel sensed the need was rather urgent. Heath slowed and turned, pulling up in front of the Frontier lobby.

"We're here." Trina tried the door but had to wait for Joel to open it for them. "I'll take Ben inside if you grab our things."

"No problem." He glanced around, not liking the way several people gawked at them. It wasn't every day that a police car dropped off two adults, a child, and a dog.

Royal bounded out, then headed to the closest bush to get busy. Joel took the suitcase, backpack, and computer case from Heath. "Thanks for the ride. I'd appreciate being kept in the loop on your investigation."

"You, Sergeant Howell, our captain, and the chief of police," Heath muttered. "Everyone in the department wants answers, and so far we don't know squat."

Not exactly reassuring, but he didn't let his disappointment show. He'd call Griff while they waited for Justin and Trevor. There had to be a way to nail this guy.

"Come, Royal." Joel waited until his K9 joined him, then headed into the hotel lobby. He stood off to the side, waiting for Trina and Ben. Ben came out of the bathrooms first, running over. "Does this place have a pool?"

"Sorry, Ben, but we're not staying here." He felt bad when the kid's expression fell. "How about we stop and get a video game for you? Will that work?"

"Okay." Ben bent to pet Royal. "Can we take him for a walk?"

"Maybe later." He couldn't agree to a walk until he knew where they were staying. Traveling with an eight-year-old added a layer of complexity to the plan. Most rental properties had a television, but would that include pay channels? He had no idea.

Trina crossed the lobby to join them. Dark circles smudged her eyes, and her expression was grim. The stress of these attacks clearly weighed heavily on her slim shoulders. "Okay, what's the plan?"

He frowned at his watch. "I'm afraid we have almost a half hour to wait before my brothers get here. We can sit in the lobby for a while." He glanced over to where a male desk clerk eyed them curiously, as if expecting them to head over to check in. "Hopefully, they won't kick us out."

"Just tell them you're a Sullivan." Trina dropped into the closest chair, raking her hands through her hair. Ben sat on the floor beside Royal. "I'm sure they won't mind."

"Very funny." His family was well known in the area, so she was probably right. But he'd much rather fly under the radar moving forward. The gunman clearly knew Joel was trying to keep Trina and Ben safe.

And he didn't seem to care if Joel or his K9 got caught in the crossfire.

His phone rang. His twin's name popped up on the screen. "Hey, Justin, where are you?"

"Fifteen minutes out," his brother said. "Where are you?"

"We're at the Frontier, but I don't plan to stay. I'd rather go someplace outside the city limits."

"I figured you might want to head somewhere off-grid, so I asked Kendra to find a rental property. She was able to secure a three-bedroom cabin north of Cody, not far from Sage Creek."

"Amenities?"

"Satellite TV and internet," Justin confirmed. "I told Kendra to go ahead and book it."

"Sounds good. We'll see you soon." He lowered the phone, catching Trina's gaze. "We have a place north of the city."

"Great."

"Can I have a snack?" Ben looked toward the vending machines that were located in the far corner of the lobby.

"Sure." He dug out his still-damp wallet and removed several bills. The kid jumped to his feet and eagerly headed over. After a moment, Royal scrambled to his feet and followed.

Trina frowned. "You shouldn't give him everything he wants."

"I get that, but after everything he's been through since this morning, I figured it was okay to make an exception." He reached for her hand and tugged her to her feet. "My sister Kendra rented a three-bedroom cabin for us. I'm sure we'll be safe there."

"I hope so." She squeezed his hand. "I wish the police would find this guy already."

"Me too." He longed to pull her into his arms, especially now that Ben was distracted by his snacks. When his phone rang again, he wanted to groan, but seeing Griff's name on the screen, he quickly answered it. "Hey, Griff. Please tell me you have something."

Trina leaned closer, obviously anxious to hear the news too.

"Well, I don't know if I would say it's good news," his future brother-in-law said. "But I think we can take Brian Ashland's name off the suspect list."

That surprised him, and by the look of shock in Trina's eyes, she found it hard to believe too. "Why is that? I'm not sure I'm willing to believe some girlfriend of his providing a half-baked alibi."

"Not a girlfriend, this alibi is one we can't ignore," Griff said. "Brian Ashland was in a bar fight two weeks ago on a Saturday night, and the judge sentenced him to thirty days in jail. Just to be sure, I called to verify that he's still locked up." Griff paused for a moment, then added, "Sorry, but he's not your guy."

"I guess that's sort of good news." He would rather have learned Brian Ashland was missing in action. By the disappointment etched on Trina's features, she felt the same way. "What about Peter Thomas?"

"The cops in Laramie haven't found him yet," Griff admitted. "They have a cop watching his apartment. I'm sure they'll pick him up soon."

"Unless he's here in Cody," Trina whispered.

"What was that?" Griff asked.

"We were just saying that Peter Thomas could be in Cody," he repeated for Griff's benefit. "You heard about the fire alarm being pulled at the hotel and that we were targeted by gunfire when we left the building?"

"Yeah, Justin filled me in." Another pause, then, "I don't like it, Joel. He's escalating big time."

"Tell me something I don't know." He glanced over to check on Ben and Royal, smiling wryly when it was clear the kid was still trying to decide which snacks to buy. "Hence why we're heading to a rental property."

"Good idea," Griff said. "I'll fill the Cody PD in on the news of Brian Ashland. That way they can focus their efforts on finding Peter Thomas."

"Thanks, Griff." He lowered the phone and ended the call. "You heard, right? Brian Ashland isn't our guy."

"I heard." Trina's brow furrowed. "I guess that helps to a certain extent. But what if the shooter isn't Peter Thomas? What if this is some other weirdo who is carrying some ridiculous grudge against me?"

"You mean like a fan of your books?" He wasn't sure he was following her thought process.

"Maybe. I don't know." She shook her head. "I was hoping for something definitive."

He slid his arm around her waist, giving her a quick, friendly hug. "Hey, don't stress. I'm sure Thomas is responsible, and having a place to start leads me to hope the police will find him very soon."

"Okay." He was encouraged at her attempt to remain positive. Then she added, "You know, I'm surprised to hear Brian is in jail. I knew he hit Evie a few times, which is why she divorced him, but apparently, his anger really has gotten out of control for him to end up with a thirty-day court-mandated sentence."

"He should do longer if you ask me." Any guy who would hit a woman in anger deserved to be behind bars.

"Well, his temper caught up to him, didn't it?" She sighed heavily and leaned against him. He tightened his grip around her waist, wishing there was more he could do to help her. "Although to be honest, I knew Brian didn't want Ben."

The citrusy scent of her hair was a distraction. He hadn't noticed it before, but he was tempted to lean in to inhale deeply, filling his head with her intriguing scent. What was it about Trina that was so attractive? She was a friend, not a potential date. He forced himself to ignore the awareness that simmered between them. "And you think Peter does?"

She shrugged. "I think Peter wants money."

He pulled away to look down into her eyes. "Okay, but it's not like he's made a kidnapping attempt to ask you for a ransom. And Ben wouldn't go along with him, even if he tried that."

"I know." She held his gaze. "It's killing me that none of this makes any sense. Shooting, starting a fire, pulling the fire alarm to shoot again. It seems like some crazy person has decided to make my life miserable."

He wondered if she was right about the person being mentally unbalanced. He had to admit, there was absolutely no sense of logic in the attacks against them. "Maybe Peter has lost his grip on reality."

"That's what I'm afraid of. I can't lose Ben." Her voice was low and tortured. "Please, Joel, promise me you'll continue to keep Ben safe. The way you did today, grabbing him and rushing him out of harm's way."

"I promise." It wasn't an easy vow to make. He cared about Trina, too, more than he should. And Royal was his responsibility as well. But when the bullets had started flying, his instincts had taken over. Protecting Ben first and foremost. "I'm not leaving you and Ben until we nail this guy."

"Thank you." Tears welled in her eyes, and then she caught him completely off guard by closing the distance between them and going up on her tippy toes to kiss him.

7

───────

Trina felt the impact of kissing Joel all the way down to her toes. It wasn't as if she hadn't kissed a man before, but this felt different. She wanted to stay in his arms forever.

"I got a candy bar!" Ben's shout had her breaking off their embrace. Her cheeks went hot as she realized what she'd done. It wasn't like her to initiate a kiss, especially not with Joel Sullivan! A man who could have any woman he wanted.

"Great!" She turned her attention to Ben, hoping Joel wouldn't notice her blush. She needed to stop thinking about him as a possible date. "Be careful that you don't make a mess."

"I won't." Ben had already opened the candy bar, chocolate smearing his fingers. After a moment, he held it out to her. "Do you want a bite?"

"No, but thank you." She was touched by his offer to share. "When you're finished, you need to wash your hands."

"I'll go with you," Joel offered. He turned to Royal. "Stay."

The dog thumped his tail on the floor as if in agreement.

She shot him a grateful glance. He didn't look nearly as impacted by her kiss, which told her all she needed to know. She harbored no illusions about her attractiveness. Her straight red hair refused to hold a curl or any sort of attempt to style it. She despised the freckles on her nose and knew she carried an extra five pounds from too much desk time at her computer. She preferred keeping to herself, rather than interacting with the world. Joel was her opposite in every way.

Whatever. It didn't matter.

Ben finished his candy bar, licking the chocolate from his fingers. Joel rested his hand on the boy's shoulder. "Let's go clean up."

Trina watched them go, realizing Ben needed a male role model to look up to. The boy clearly hadn't liked Peter, and she wasn't sure he had a lot of good memories about his father either.

Yet it wasn't as if Joel had volunteered for the job. This was a temporary interlude. The danger that stalked her had thrown them together. It was more important than ever to stay focused on Ben.

Her nephew was all that mattered.

Royal stared in the direction Joel had gone. She was reassured by the dog's presence. At the very least, Royal would alert her to danger. She dragged her fingers through her fine red hair, forcing a smile as Ben and Joel returned to the lobby.

Royal jumped up to join them, as if Joel had been gone hours instead of minutes.

"Good boy." Joel bent to stroke the dog's silky fur. "My brothers will be here soon. If you don't mind, I'd like to pick up a replacement video game for Ben."

"Really? Can we?" Ben asked hopefully.

Irked that Joel had brought it up in front of the boy, she reluctantly nodded. She'd let it slide this time, mostly because they'd need something to keep Ben distracted at the rental property. But Joel needed to understand he couldn't set her up like that moving forward. Ben was going through a lot, but that didn't mean she intended to give in to his every whim.

"Just one." She kept her gaze stern. "No whining, okay?"

"I won't." Ben turned and ran across the lobby, nearly bumping into a couple who were trying to check in. Royal stood as if to join in, but Joel kept him back with a hand on his collar.

"Ben, watch where you're going." She had learned over the past few weeks that Ben had boundless energy. Too bad she didn't.

"Sorry." Ben ducked around the couple. Thankfully, they didn't seem to mind.

Joel's phone rang. "Hey, Justin. Yep, sounds good." He pocketed the phone and turned to her. "We'll use the side exit to meet Justin around back."

"Sounds good to me. Come, Ben." Before she could reach for the suitcase, Joel grabbed it.

Leaving him to it, she shouldered her laptop case. At this rate, she wasn't going to meet her deadline. Not that she couldn't ask for a few extra days if needed, but it was a point of pride that she'd always met her deadlines.

Even with everything going on with her sister's death, she'd managed to get her writing finished.

Maybe she could use some of this in her next book. She followed Joel and Royal down the hallway. Ben skipped over to join them. "Are we gonna buy my video game now?"

"Soon." She had no idea when Joel planned to stop. Then she realized they'd likely need groceries as a cabin wouldn't have room service. No doubt they'd pick up whatever they needed here in Cody, before heading to the rental property.

Outside the sun was hot as they crossed the parking lot to a pair of twin black SUVs stood idling. As they approached, the respective driver's side doors opened, and two young, fit men stepped out. The rear hatches lifted, too, and two dogs jumped down. Royal ran over to greet what appeared to be two more labs, one yellow, the other with a reddish-brown coat.

She recognized Justin, Joel's twin. She didn't remember Trevor as well but smiled in greeting as both Sullivans stepped forward.

"Nice to see you, Trina." Justin gave her a nod and tossed the key fob to Joel, who caught it easily. "This SUV is yours. Stone and I will head back with Trev."

"Hi, Trina." Trevor greeted her with a wide smile. "I remember you from high school."

He did? That statement flustered her. She managed to smile back. "Nice to see you and Justin again. I'm sorry to have caused you to drive all this way."

"No problem." Justin waved that aside. "We're happy to help."

"You better call Chase," Trevor warned. "He heard about—ah, everything."

She appreciated his understanding that Ben was listening in. Although in truth, Ben was preoccupied with watching the dogs. The look of longing on the boy's face was difficult to ignore.

"I will." Joel didn't look concerned about his older brother's wrath. "I spoke to Griff, that should be good enough."

"You know how Chase is." Trevor shrugged. "Our oldest brother takes our safety seriously."

"Here's the information on the rental property." Justin showed Joel his phone. "I'll text you the information Kendra provided."

"Thanks." Joel nodded as the text popped up on his screen. "Kendra is a whizz at this stuff."

"Yeah, she spends a lot of time on that computer when she's not doing SAR work with Smoky." Trevor frowned. "I think she's digging into the pilot's background."

Trina cocked her head. "What pilot?"

"The pilot of the plane that crashed into the mountains with our parents on board." Joel scowled. "Does Chase know that?"

"Not sure. But she hasn't found much yet, so it probably doesn't matter." Trevor turned to the dogs. "Archie, come."

The rust-colored dog wheeled and trotted to Trevor's side.

"Come, Stone," Justin called. The yellow lab followed suit; his tongue hanging out of his mouth made the dog look happy. She was impressed all over again by how well trained the Sullivan K9s were. She wondered if Joel would help her and Ben train their puppy.

Then she reminded herself that he'd be too busy for that. Besides, it wasn't as if she needed a dog trained to do search and rescue. She and Ben would manage, just like millions of other pet owners across the globe.

And maybe she could incorporate the puppy into her mystery series. Her main character had a cat, and adding a dog might provide another aspect to the story.

"Thanks for coming out." Joel opened the back passenger door to set the suitcase inside. She stepped forward to put the laptop bag on the floor too.

"Stay in touch." Justin gestured to the car. "By the way, we stuck a satellite phone in the back just in case the cell service is spotty."

"Sounds good. I had forgotten to grab one when I headed to Cody." Joel paused, then added, "Are you sticking around until the SUV has been towed to the garage for repair?"

"Yep." Trevor tucked his hands into his front pockets. "Don't worry, we'll take care of it."

"Appreciate that." Joel turned to face her. "Ready to go?"

"Sure." She stepped closer to Ben who was

kneeling beside Royal, lavishing the dog with attention. "Thanks again, Justin and Trevor."

The Sullivan brothers nodded, keeping their dogs at their sides as Joel loaded Royal in the back crate area. She waited for Ben to climb into the back seat, then went around to the passenger-side door.

Moments later, they were back on the road.

"Don't forget my video game," Ben called from the back.

The corner of Joel's mouth curved in a smile. "I won't. We'll get food too," he added.

"Okay." Trina tried to relax, despite knowing the danger was far from over. She noticed Joel eyed the rearview mirror often as he navigated the streets of the city.

An hour later, they had enough groceries to feed them for a week and a replacement handheld video game for Ben. She'd tried to pay for their purchases, but Joel refused.

"Let me do this, Trina." He kept his voice low. "You and Ben have been through a lot. I want to help."

She knew better than to read into his kindness but choked up just the same. When they finally reached the cabin, she was surprised at how nice it was.

As they carried everything inside, she tried not to imagine what it would be like to have someone like Joel helping her with Ben on a regular basis. Then she sternly reminded herself that this was not her life.

But she was still secretly glad Joel had insisted on staying with her and Ben until this assailant was caught and arrested.

~

KEENLY AWARE OF Trina and Ben exploring the cabin, Joel busied himself with putting food away. A place like this was far better than a hotel, but it also made things seem—more intimate between them.

He noticed his brothers had included a laptop computer too. A good thing because he needed to try to figure out who was behind these attacks. Doing nothing wasn't his strong suit. Back home, there was always a myriad of chores that needed to be done.

Royal sniffed the cabin with interest.

Subtly checking his phone, he was reassured to see there was cell service. A good thing, as he wanted to check in with Griff. And he should probably call Chase too.

When he noticed that Trina had rolled her suitcase down the short hallway toward the bedrooms, he called, "Take the master suite. You deserve to have your own bathroom."

"Okay, thanks." She waved a hand at their surroundings. "I didn't expect anything this nice. It's kind of luxurious, isn't it?"

He shrugged. To his mind, the place was nice enough but not extravagant. "It's a rental. People expect to stay in a nice place when renting a place in the mountains."

"I guess I was expecting a rustic hunting type of place." She flashed a quick smile, then continued down the hall, calling, "Ben, come pick your room."

The boy jumped off the sofa and ran down the hall. Royal trotted after them. Joel smiled, glad the dog would have a playmate for a while.

When Joel had finished putting stuff away, he reached for his phone. Griff answered on the first ring. "Hey, Griff. Have you learned anything new?"

"Not yet. The Laramie PD still have not located Peter Thomas." Griff paused, then added, "They're starting to wonder if you're right about him being involved in this."

"Did you mention the information about how Evie loaned him money?" Joel asked. "That may play into his motive."

"I did. That was new information for them, and they're taking it seriously," Griff assured him. "I've been digging into Trina's boyfriends; they're all still in the area. I figure I'll head out to interview them in person."

It bothered Joel to be sitting there while Griff did the legwork. But he also had no intention of leaving Trina and Ben here alone. "Will you let me know how that goes?"

"Yep." Another pause, then Griff said, "You'd better call Chase. He's annoyed to be the last to know about the danger you've landed in."

"I'm not the one in danger." He sighed, then added, "I'll call him. But Chase isn't one to talk. He didn't tell any of us about Eli's kidnapping until he needed additional resources."

"I know all about that. I was there, remember?" Griff said. "I'm just the messenger."

"Understood." Joel knew his future brother-in-law didn't deserve his frustration. "I have computer access here. What can I do to help?"

"I've already done background checks. You can try social media, but otherwise, there isn't anything I can think of."

That was not what he wanted to hear. He cast a quick glance around the room. "Griff, I seriously need something to do. Anything."

"I'll think about it and let you know. Right now, I need to hit the road so I can talk to these former boyfriends. We'll chat more later, okay?" Griff ended the call without giving him a chance to respond.

"Great. Fine." He muttered to himself as he set

his phone aside. "I'll just sit here twiddling my thumbs."

"The bedroom across from the master suite is yours." Trina glanced out at the wooded lot surrounding the cabin. "Is it safe for Ben to go outside for a while? He'd like to play with Royal."

"Sure, that's no problem." He'd made sure they weren't followed. Granted, he'd done that on the way to the Elk Lodge. He secretly hoped Peter or whoever was responsible for these attacks was wasting time checking out the other hotels in the area.

"Thanks." Trina turned to Ben. "You can take Royal outside, but don't go too far. You don't want to get lost in these woods, right?"

"Right." Ben nodded solemnly, then grinned. "Let's go, Royal!"

Ben darted to the front door. Royal followed, then paused to look at Joel as if asking permission. He nodded at his K9. "Go ahead."

Royal wagged his tail and followed Ben outside. Ben let the door slam shut loudly behind him. Then his voice, shouted, "Sorry!"

Trina chuckled. "That kid."

"He's fine." Going out to play in the woods was something all young boys liked to do. "Royal will keep an eye on him."

"I know. I have to say, that's a huge relief. Otherwise, I'd feel the need to be out there with him." She tucked a strand of her red-gold hair behind her ear. "I don't know how Evie took care of Ben while working a full-time job. It's exhausting."

"I'm sure things will get easier over time." He was only guessing since he didn't have any kids of his own and couldn't imagine what it was like to become a parent to an eight-year-old overnight. "Especially when school starts."

"To be honest, I'm looking forward to that." She flushed. "It's not that I don't love Ben, but I am seriously behind on writing this book. Writing while he's at school sounds heavenly." She grimaced, then asked, "Do you mind if I work for a bit?"

"Not at all. Go for it." He wasn't about to stand in her way.

"Thanks." She sat on the sofa and opened her laptop case. Minutes later, her gaze was focused on the screen, fingers flying across the keyboard. He watched in awe, as it seemed as if she'd picked up exactly where she'd left off without a problem.

How she could write one book, let alone a few, was amazing to him. Leaving her to it, he turned his attention to mining social media.

Trina had mentioned Peter hadn't posted anything on social media since Evie's death. He had trouble finding the correct account, then carried the computer to the sofa. "Sorry to bother you, can you just verify if this is the correct Peter Thomas?"

"Huh?" She blinked at him, as if needing a moment to switch gears. Then she leaned forward to look at the screen. "Yes, that's the one. But why are you looking at it? We already know he's not posted anything recently."

"It's something to do." He shrugged and turned away. "I can't sit here doing nothing."

"I get that." She watched him for a moment, then looked back at the screen. "I just want to finish this scene."

"That's not a problem." He felt bad for interrupting and imagined she dealt with a lot of that from Ben.

Determined to keep quiet, he scrolled through some of the messages that had been left by friends of Peter. One name in particular caught his eye. A woman by the name of Casey Mueller seemed concerned that she hadn't heard from Peter. She left several comments on his last post, asking him to call her.

He frowned, seeing three of the same comment one right after the other. In a way, they reminded him of Lisa's persistence. Which now that he thought about it, she hadn't bothered him since that call earlier in the morning. Still, it was enough to make him wonder about the relationship between

Peter and this Casey. Had Peter cheated on Evie prior to her death? Or was he reading more into a concerned message than he ought to? Guys could have female friends, and there was nothing in her message to indicate they had been more than pals.

Still, he copied the name down, hoping to run it past Griff. Then he clicked to see Casey's page. He could only see her profile page, nothing more, so he went back to reading the comments on Peter's page.

Nothing else stood out to him as being significant. Casey was the only one who seemed to have noticed that Peter hadn't posted anything recently. He decided to switch gears to find Brian Ashland's information.

Griff had confirmed Brian was in jail, so he couldn't have carried out the attacks against Trina. That was fine, but maybe the guy had hired someone else to do the dirty work. It was a stretch. Joel doubted the guy was rolling in money, as they already knew he had credit card debt. Yet it was worth a look.

Besides, he had nothing better to do.

He paused to cross over to the window. Ben and Royal were in the yard, Ben had a stick in his hand, and he was waving it around like a sword. He and Justin had done the same thing as kids. Once Justin had nearly poked Joel's eye out. Their mother had not been amused when Joel had come into the house bleeding from a deep scratch near his left eye. He had to smile at how Ben was fighting imaginary foes. Deciding the boy was fine, he returned to the computer.

Trina hadn't even looked up, working intensely as if lost in her thoughts. Or in her fictional Montana town.

She hadn't confided in him about her pseudonym, so he couldn't check out her web page or her books. He wasn't sure why he was so curious and forced himself to go back to searching on Brian's social media pages.

That proved to be a fruitless effort too. He couldn't find anything on Brian and decided the guy must have purposefully stayed low-key to avoid paying child support. Trina had mentioned that her sister hadn't pursued the issue, but if she had, the court would have garnished the guy's wages.

What a loser. No surprise he'd ended up in jail.

Joel pushed away from the computer, feeling restless. Why would Brian bother to attack Trina? Unless he thought that Trina might force the issue of child support. He turned, intending to run that theory past Trina, then caught himself. She was engrossed in her work. Since he had no idea how long it would take her to write a scene, he stood and walked to the window overlooking the backyard instead.

He frowned, not seeing Ben or Royal. He wasn't that worried; Royal would sound the alarm if there was a problem. But Trina had told the boy to stay close.

Not that he and his twin had listened very well at that age.

He moved to another window, overlooking the side of the cabin. When there was still no sign of Ben, he wandered down the hall to the bedrooms.

After verifying the kid wasn't playing within sight of the cabin, he returned to the main room. "I'm heading out to check on Ben."

"Hmmm." Trina barely looked up from her screen. She was cute, gnawing her lower lip while working.

Hiding a smile, he slipped outside. He walked a few feet from the cabin, searching the woods for a sign of the boy. "Ben? Where are you? You were supposed to stay close to the cabin, remember?"

There was no response, so he strode to the last place he'd seen the boy. "Ben!" His tone was sharp now. "Get back here."

"Coming!" Ben's voice sounded faint, as if he were farther away than Joel had anticipated.

Royal emitted a low growl seconds before he heard a grunting sound. The tiny hairs on the back of his neck rose in alarm. He recognized that sound as coming from a grizzly bear.

"Ben!" He shouted the boy's name as he bolted into the woods. "Stay where you are! Don't move!" He feared the boy must have gotten between a mama bear and her cub. Grizzlies didn't attack without a reason. The two biggest reasons a grizzly would lash out were if they were protecting a food source or their cubs.

Royal's growls grew louder, then the dog let out a series of sharp barks. Joel quickly drew the weapon from his belt holster, praying the grizzly would turn away.

He didn't want to put the bear down if he didn't have to.

"Joel? I see a bear!" Ben's voice held a mixture of fear and awe. "It's huge!"

Dear Lord Jesus, protect him! "Stay where you are. Don't move any closer, understand?"

Royal's barking continued, and the grunting sound from the bear grew into a roar. Joel ducked under branches, desperate to reach Ben and Royal. He knew the dog would plant himself between Ben and the bear, sacrificing his life if necessary.

"Yah! Yah!" Joel saw the brown grizzly bear now, and it was massive. A female, most likely. There was no sign of a radio collar around its neck. Many of the bears in Yellowstone National Park were tracked by the DNR but not all of them. Joel waved his arms over his head, yelling as loudly as possible. "Go, scat! Go away!"

The bear reared up on its hind legs and roared again. The sound sent chills down his spine. In all the years he'd been doing search and rescue, he'd never been this close to a grizzly.

"Ben, get behind me. Don't run, walk slowly backward toward me. Royal, heel." He continued waving his arms as he spoke, praying the bear would turn away. If it made a single move toward them, he'd have no choice but to shoot.

Thankfully, the bear's roars had scared Ben into shocked silence. The boy walked backward, then tripped over a log, hitting the ground hard. The abrupt movement made the bear roar loudly again.

"Yah! Yah!" Joel screamed at the bear as he hurried forward to stand in front of Ben. When the bear didn't back down, he brought his arms down and held the gun with two hands. He swallowed and tried to calm his racing heart. A handgun wasn't always powerful enough to drop a bear in its tracks.

He'd have to hit the beast square in the heart or head. And he could not afford to miss.

There was a rustling sound from the area beyond the bear, and for a horrible moment, Joel feared the mate was nearby. Male and female bears didn't usually travel together, but anything was possible.

Then he saw the brown fur of a smaller bear. The grizzly's cub.

After another long moment, the bear turned toward the cub. Joel kept his weapon trained on the beast until it had lumbered away, with the cub running alongside.

He lowered his arms, let out a deep sigh, and glanced gratefully at the sky overhead. *Thank You, Lord Jesus!*

That had been far too close.

8

———————

A thundering roar pierced the air, pulling Trina from her story. At first she thought she imagined the sound, along with the frantic barking of a dog. Then the tiny hairs on the back of her neck rose when she heard the roar again. It was a ferocious sound, one she'd never heard before in her twenty-eight years.

Tossing her laptop aside, she jumped up and bolted outside. She thought she heard a deep voice yelling, too, but couldn't figure out where it was coming from. "Ben? Joel?" She scanned the clearing around the cabin, her heart thundering in her chest. There was no sign of Ben, Joel, or Royal.

The three of them had to be together, but what happened? Where were they? What animal had made that awful sound?

"Ben!" She couldn't hide the desperate fear in her voice. Which way should she go to try to find them? She wasn't the search and rescue expert, Joel was! And where was Royal? "Ben! Where are you?"

Now there was nothing but silence, which was oddly more frightening than the roar. Was it over? Were they all dead?

No! Please, no!

"Ben!" she shouted again.

After what seemed like a lifetime, but was only a few seconds, she heard Joel's calm voice. "We're okay, just stay where you are, we're coming to you."

Coming from where? She turned in a full circle, trying to pinpoint where his voice originated. The woods surrounding the cabin were pretty, but now she'd have given anything to be back in Cody with lots of people surrounding them.

Not whatever wild animal had made that disturbing noise.

"Aunt Trina!" Ben broke free of the woods to her left. She turned and hurried forward to meet him. He threw himself into her arms, and she clutched him close. "It was huge!" Reaction must have set in because Ben's shoulders shook, his voice muffled against her chest. "Biggest ever."

"It's okay. You're safe now" She tried not to let her own panic break through. She hadn't seen any blood on Ben, so she had to believe he wasn't physically hurt.

Joel and Royal emerged a moment later. The grave expression on Joel's face worried her more than anything else could have. If he had been scared, she understood the situation had been dire. "What was it?"

"A bear!" Ben's arms clamped tighter around her waist. "Aunt Trina, it was a giant bear!"

"It was big, but we're okay." Joel's calm voice wasn't as reassuring as she'd have liked. "Mama grizzly was protecting her cub. Somehow, Ben and Royal got too close."

A grizzly? Of all the wildlife in the area, grizzly bears were by far the most dangerous. Knowledge she'd only gotten through books, not firsthand experience. Her mouth went dry. "How did you get away?"

Joel somberly shook his head. "I'm not sure. One minute I was aiming to shoot her in the heart, the next she turned and ambled off."

He'd almost been forced to shoot! Her knees threatened to buckle, but she managed to stay upright. "I can't believe this."

"Yeah, it was not a great situation. Let's get inside," Joel suggested. "I think we've had enough outside time."

"Agree." She leaned back, trying to see Ben's face. "Hey, are you okay?"

The boy nodded and finally loosened his grip around her waist. When he looked up at her, his red eyes betrayed his tears. His voice wobbled a bit as he said, "That was scary."

"I'm sure it was." She tried to take her cue from Joel, who'd obviously been concerned about the seriousness of their predicament but hadn't shown it. At least, not to Ben. No wonder Royal had been barking. The dog was calm now, though, which was a good sign. With forced cheerfulness, she said, "Why don't we see what's on television?"

Ben nodded but stayed close to her side as they turned to head into the cabin. Joel came up behind her, holding the door for them.

"Find the remote, Ben." She knew her nephew would have better luck understanding how to use it than she would. "See if you can find a good station."

Ben headed into the living room to find the remote, with Royal on his heels. She grabbed Joel's arm and tugged him into the kitchen. "What on earth happened?"

He grimaced. "I heard the bear grunt in warning. Royal barked, but Ben didn't seem to understand the danger. Somehow, Ben had gotten too close to her bear cub. By the time I got there, well, the bear was in full protection mode. She roared and went up on her hind legs to intimidate us."

She swallowed hard, trying not to imagine what would have happened if Joel hadn't gotten there in time. "She would have attacked Ben."

"Probably." Joel nodded to where Royal was stretched out on the sofa beside Ben. "Royal stood protectively between the grizzly and Ben."

"That's all fine and dandy, but the dog would have died too. Just like Ben." She closed her eyes for a moment, trying not to lose it. She took one deep breath, then another. She finally looked at him. "I can't believe Ben stumbled across a bear."

"I know. It was a close call." Joel lightly touched her arm. "God was looking out for us today. It's the only explanation for why I wasn't forced to shoot her. A few seconds longer and I would have taken her down."

Her brief flash of anger faded as she understood Joel would have sacrificed himself to protect Ben. "Thank you."

He shrugged. "Like I said, God was watching over us today."

Maybe he was right. Just remembering that roaring was enough to make her blood run cold. With a few swipes of her bear paws, that mama bear could have killed Ben and Royal in seconds.

Joel too.

"I'm glad God was watching over us." She tried to smile. "But I would rather not repeat that experience anytime soon." She didn't add the thought that they'd come to the cabin to be safe from the gunman, not to be mauled by a grizzly.

"Have to say, that was a first for me." Joel shook his head ruefully. "I've seen bears from afar, but not up close and personal like that."

"Thanks again for protecting Ben."

"Always." He tucked his hands into the front pockets of his jeans. Joel was so handsome, she wanted nothing more than to step into his arms, reliving their brief yet powerful kiss. Instead, she turned away from the temptation. She needed to be strong. Leaning on Joel for comfort and support wasn't smart. Doing that would only make it more difficult to move on with her life alone once he was gone.

And she had no illusions about the chances of their friendship turning into something more. Joel was a great guy—sweet, caring, and protective. But he would never be satisfied with a dull and boring homebody like her. Someone who lived her adventures through her storytelling, not by doing them herself.

Besides, she was a single mother now and needed to stay focused on providing a loving home for Ben. Her personal life wasn't important.

"I, ah, should think about dinner." Another part of her life that had changed since taking guardianship of Ben. Living alone, she hadn't necessarily kept to a specific schedule regarding meals. If her writing was going well, she'd go with the flow. But the books she'd read about parenting suggested kids did best with a scheduled routine. Glancing at her watch now, she realized it was close to five.

"I can handle that," Joel offered. "We bought the fixings for spaghetti, right?"

"Yes, Ben's favorite."

"Great. We'll have that tonight." Joel gestured toward the living room. "Why don't you try to finish your scene?"

She flushed, amazed that he'd even mentioned her work. Robby had treated her livelihood more like a hobby than a job. As if she made money without putting forth an effort. Ben, too, hadn't really seemed to understand that her time at the computer generated her income stream. Joel's offer to cook was sweet. Yet she'd just lectured herself on not leaning on him. "I can handle making dinner."

He frowned. "I know you're capable of that and more. But I don't mind. I'd rather cook, if that's okay. I'm used to being busy."

That she could believe. Joel wasn't the type to sit around doing nothing. Maybe she was doing him a favor, rather than leaning on him. Still, she hesitated. "Are you sure?"

"Yep. I've got this." He pushed away from the counter. "Go do your thing."

Suddenly tears pricked at her eyes, which was ridiculous since she hadn't been the one in danger. His kind understanding wasn't a reason to become overly emotional. What was wrong with her anyway? She needed to stop being foolish. Subtly brushing the moisture away, she crossed over to grab her computer. Ben sat on the sofa with Royal curled up beside him. With one hand on the dog, Ben used the remote to flip through the seemingly endless stream of stations.

Leaving him to it, she carried her laptop to the recliner. She had been close to finishing her scene, which was why it had taken a moment for the bear's roar to penetrate her brain. Now she reviewed what she'd written and picked up her train of thought.

She finished her scene, then went back to read what she'd written to make sure it made sense. It was only then that she realized the way she'd described the local sheriff of her fictional Montana town was a man who looked exactly like Joel Sullivan.

Shaking her head at her foolishness, she closed the laptop. Another reason why she wouldn't tell Joel her pseudonym. The last thing she wanted was for him to realize the extent of her ridiculous childhood crush.

~

AFTER WASHING up at the sink, Joel began making dinner. The close encounter with mama grizzly had shaken him more than he cared to admit. Describing the event to Trina had only reinforced how close Ben had come to being hurt. Or worse.

His biggest concern was that Ben hadn't recognized the danger until it was too late. The boy hadn't understood the grunting sound as a warning. And worse, Ben hadn't picked up on Royal's reaction either. His K9 had set off the alarm, barking to alert Ben of the impending danger.

He glanced over to where the kid was watching television. He and his siblings had grown up on the ranch. Joel had learned about how to recognize and deal with wildlife at a very young age. Chase had spent a lot of time hunting and fishing, eventually opening his own guide business. Chase had learned everything he knew from their father.

Obviously, Ben hadn't experienced a similar upbringing. Joel would need to spend some time with Ben in the woods, teaching him about the various signs of danger. Like the bear scat Joel had noticed once the danger had passed.

Finding fresh bear scat should have put anyone nearby on high alert. And if he'd been there to see it first, he'd have made sure Ben avoided that area.

When he finished browning the ground beef, he added the spaghetti sauce, then set about making noodles. His phone rang, and seeing Chase's name on the screen, he silently groaned as he answered.

"Why haven't you called me?" his brother demanded.

"Hey, Chase, how are you?" Joel kept his voice calm. He moved off to the side so his voice wouldn't carry into the living room. "You talked to Griff, right?"

"Yes, but I'd like to hear what's going on from you." Chase's sarcastic tone made him wince. "You told Anna you were helping a friend, not that you were smack in the middle of danger."

"To be fair, Trina and her nephew, Ben, are the ones in danger, not me." Joel knew his eldest brother was protective of them, especially the younger siblings. "I'm just trying to keep them both safe."

"Which puts you in the middle of danger." Chase's voice rose in anger. "Come on, Joel, be straight with me. What's going on?"

"I honestly wish I knew," Joel admitted, cutting his older brother some slack. "That's why I called Griff for help. Trina's sister died in a mountain bike accident at the end of May. She has guardianship of her eight-year-old nephew, Ben. At first we thought Ben's father was the one doing this, but he happens to be serving a short stint in jail for assault and battery. There's another former boyfriend of her sister who the cops are still trying to locate."

"An eight-year-old, huh?" Joel knew his brother was thinking of his five-year-old son, Eli. "That's not good."

"Exactly why I'm here." Joel sighed. "I'm sorry I didn't call; things have been a little hairy over here. Ben stumbled upon a mama grizzly protecting her cub."

"Oh man." Chase let out a low whistle. "Did you have to put her down?"

"No, but it was a close call." He glanced over to where Trina was engrossed in her laptop computer. "Can't say I've ever been that close to a mad grizzly before. Thankfully, everything turned out fine. I do think Ben could use some wilderness training."

"Every kid should," Chase agreed. "So you really have no clue who's behind these attacks?"

"Not yet." He filled his brother in on Peter Thomas. "He's our top suspect. Hey, is Griff around? He was heading out to interview some of Trina's former boyfriends."

"Not that I'm aware of, but Rocky and I just got back from a search ourselves." Chase sighed loudly.

"It's crazy how many calls we're taking. Anna is worried we're going to end up turning people away if things don't calm down."

"Sorry to be out of the rotation." Joel kept an eye on the kettle of water that needed to boil. "I'm hoping Peter Thomas is our perp. If so, it shouldn't take the Laramie and Cody PD to find and arrest him."

"I hope so. But promise to keep me in the loop going forward." Chase made the request sound like an order.

It was tempting to remind his brother that he was twenty-nine, not a kid. But he simply said, "Sure thing."

"Oh, and call if you need more backup," Chase said. "We're busy, but our family comes first."

"I will. We should be fine here at the cabin Kendra found for us. Later, Chase." He ended the call and set his phone aside. It was hard to stay angry at his oldest brother considering how Chase and his sister Maya had never hesitated to give up their personal lives and careers to return to the ranch after their parents died. Joel knew the siblings had grown closer during that time, especially when Maya had come up with the idea of changing the luxury dude ranch into a mission of search and rescue.

Months of training had brought them even

closer together. Maya had already been a K9 cop, so she'd taken the lead on the dog training aspect of the plan along with the trainer she'd hired. Chase had used his hunting guide skills to make sure every one of them could survive and navigate through the wilderness using a compass.

He was glad his oldest siblings were now married and having kids. They certainly deserved to be happy. Didn't mean he was planning to head down that path.

Yet as he glanced over at Trina and Ben, he couldn't deny the weird twinge near his heart. Giving himself a mental shake, he realized the water was finally boiling. He dumped spaghetti noodles into the pot and began to stir.

"Dinner will be ready in fifteen," he called.

"Okay," Ben said, his gaze focused on the television.

"Great, thanks." Trina set her laptop aside, then came over to join him in the kitchen. "What can I do to help?"

"Nothing. It's all under control."

She opened the cupboards until she found plates and cups. "Thanks again for making dinner. I'm really glad I was able to get some work done."

"I told you, it's better for me to keep busy." Her comment made him wonder if she hadn't gotten support like this in the past. Not that he wanted details about her dating life.

"Who was on the phone?" She glanced at him questioningly as she set the table. "Did the Laramie police find Peter Thomas yet?"

"That was Chase. My oldest brother," he added at her confused look. "Maya is the oldest of all of us, then Chase. From there, it's Jessica, Shane, Alexis, me, Justin, Trevor, and Kendra."

"You're older than Justin?"

"By a full three minutes." He'd often teased Justin about being younger. As if three minutes mattered.

"I can't imagine having nine kids, but especially twins," Trina murmured.

"Yeah, I have to admit, it was a lot." He grinned. "I sometimes wondered if our parents had more kids so they could make us work the ranch. Everyone had to chip in to do chores. Justin and I ended up spending a lot of time in the barn with the horses. On the bright side, we always had someone to hang out with. That part was fun."

"You sound so close." Trina tucked her hair behind her ears. "Evie and I were close while growing up but drifted apart a bit after her marriage."

He nodded and tasted a noodle to make sure they were cooked before removing the pan from the stove. He dumped the noodles into a colander and ran cold water over them. "We grew closer after our parents died. Chase and Maya were great in keeping us together after that."

"I wish I'd been closer to Evie over the past few years." Trina sighed. "I should have moved to Laramie when she asked."

"Hey, my older siblings lived in different cities too." He didn't think there was any reason for her to feel guilty over living her life. "I don't think that's unusual."

"Maybe not." She grimaced. "Still, it would have been an easier transition for Ben if I had."

"Hindsight," he reminded her. "There's no way you could have anticipated your sister would pass away. Besides, Ben's doing fine." He gestured to the noodles. "Dinner's ready."

"Thanks." She moved past him into the living room. "Come on, Ben. It's time to eat."

"Can't I watch the end of this?" Ben barely glanced at her. "It's almost over."

"Five minutes," Trina said firmly.

"Okay."

He caught Trina's gaze. "I need to get Royal's dog food from the back of the SUV. I'll be back in a minute."

She nodded.

When Joel returned, Royal unfolded himself from the sofa, stretched, then trotted into the kitchen. Joel smiled. "You know it's dinnertime, don't you, boy?"

Royal wagged his tail, lifting his nose toward the container. Joel scooped kibble into a bowl and set it on the floor for his K9. He filled another bowl with water, then stood back for a moment. Royal sniffed the air again, then sat and stared up at him, waiting for the command.

Joel made him wait a full thirty seconds before telling him to go get it. Royal jumped up and quickly went over to eat.

"I'm impressed at how well behaved he is," Trina admitted. She turned as if to tell Ben to hurry up, but the boy was already heading to the table.

"Royal is a good boy, isn't he?" Ben reached out to stroke Royal. Thankfully, his dog wasn't food protective and didn't react in a negative manner.

Trina carried the spaghetti meat sauce and noodles to the table. Once they were seated, she looked at him expectantly. He nodded and glanced at Ben. "Put your hands together, Ben. We're going to say grace."

"Again?" Ben asked, as if confused.

"We say grace at every meal," he explained. "And when we're finished, we say, 'Amen.'"

Ben glanced at Trina as if to ask why but then nodded. "Okay."

"Lord Jesus, we ask You to bless this food we are

about to eat. We are also thankful at how You protected us today when we stumbled across the grizzly bear. We ask that You please continue to keep us all safe in Your care. Amen."

"Amen," Trina and Ben said simultaneously.

Trina served Ben first, then spooned spaghetti and noodles onto her own plate. He waited to go last, making sure there was some left over in case Trina or Ben wanted seconds.

"Yum." Ben twirled his fork in his noodles. Then he glanced up at Joel. "Do bears like spaghetti?"

"No, bears usually eat fish and berries." He glanced at Trina, and added, "But you do need to be careful about leaving food outside. Bears love sweets and will come to eat whatever you leave out."

Ben's eyes widened. "You mean that big bear might come back?"

"Only if you leave food outside." He was trying to walk the line between teaching Ben about animals and keeping him safe while not being afraid. "Normally, bears don't bother people, unless there's food nearby or if they're protecting their cub."

"A cub is a baby bear," Ben said. "We learned that in school."

"That's correct." Joel nodded. "I saw a bear cub nearby this morning, which is why that mama bear got mad at us for being too close."

Ben's expression turned thoughtful. "I didn't see a baby bear."

"I'll teach you how to recognize bear scat," Joel said. "That way you'll know to avoid bears moving forward."

Trina looked as if she wanted to argue, but when he held her gaze for a moment, she kept silent. He sensed she'd rather keep Ben inside rather than risk him running into a similar situation as he had today. The problem with that approach was that you couldn't wrap kids in bubble plastic to keep them safe.

Ben frowned. "I don't want to see another big bear."

"Exactly," Joel agreed. "If you knew how to identify bear scat, you'd know there was an animal close by and could head back home, rather than risk seeing one."

The boy considered that and nodded. "Okay. I'd like to learn that."

"Great." He took a bite of his spaghetti. It wasn't half bad, if he said so himself.

"You really think that will work?" Trina asked in a low voice.

"I do, yes." He arched a brow. "I can show you too."

She wrinkled her nose, then sighed. "Okay. I'll learn, too, then."

"We'll take a look after dinner." He figured the mama grizzly was long gone by now.

They ate in silence for several minutes. From the way Trina picked at her food, he sensed the talk about bear scat had ruined her appetite.

He was just finishing his meal when his phone rang. He rose from the table to grab the device off the counter. This time the caller was Griff, so he quickly answered, hoping for news. "Hey, Griff. How did it go?"

"Well, I was able to knock one guy off the suspect list." Griff sounded weary. "I learned from Toby's parents that he's working the rodeo in Cheyenne. Just to be sure, I contacted the rodeo organizers. Toby absolutely is working there for the entire season."

"Okay, that's good news, I guess. But what about Robby or that other guy, Luke?" Joel was most interested in Robby.

"Luke Davenport works for a river rafting company during the summer. I've left him a message but haven't heard back yet. Robby Rawlings is supposed to be working as a bartender at the Horseshoe Saloon, but he called in sick for the past two days. When I went to his apartment, nobody answered the door."

Joel frowned. "You think Robby is behind this?"

"I don't know, but according to his fellow bartender at the Horseshoe, Robby had a big blow up with his girlfriend two weeks ago. Sounds like the girlfriend told him off and that another guy had to grab Robby to keep him from slugging her." Griff's voice was flat with anger. "Rawlings clearly has anger issues."

"Just like Brian Ashland." Joel frowned. He didn't like knowing the guy hadn't been at work for the past two days. Maybe it wasn't too farfetched to think the guy was out to get revenge on those who hurt him.

Like Trina.

9

"Who's like Brian Ashland?" Trina could only hear Joel's side of the conversation, but it wasn't difficult to figure out they were discussing her former boyfriends. Joel had asked about Luke and Robby, which indicated Toby must have been in the clear. She hadn't wanted to admit to Joel that both Luke and Toby had broken things up with her.

She'd actually stayed with Robby longer than she should have because of that. At some point, she'd realized that being alone was better than sticking it out with Robby.

"Thanks, Griff. Later." Joel lowered his phone. "Robby missed work the past two days. And apparently had an argument with his girlfriend a few weeks ago." Joel's blue eyes narrowed. "Other patrons of the bar had to physically restrain him from striking her."

"That's not good." She swallowed hard. Breaking things off with Robby had been the right thing to do. "I knew he could get mad, but I never anticipated he could hit someone. Especially a woman."

"He came close, but I'm more interested in where Robby is now."

"His apartment?" she suggested.

"Griff said he didn't answer the door." Joel picked up his empty plate and carried it to the table. The little things he did, clearing his dishes, chipping in to cook and clean up, only reinforced the differences between Joel and Robby. Robby had been a slob, and since he lived in an apartment, he had liked spending time at her place.

Maybe that was the reason he was upset about her breaking things off. Robby may have imagined they'd get married, enabling him to move into her house permanently.

Despite hearing Robby had been MIA for two days, she still couldn't imagine him lashing out at her like this. In a fit of anger, yeah. But coldly positioning himself nearby for the sole purpose of shooting at her? Setting the fire?

No, she could not mesh those images in her mind.

"Has Griff said anything more about Peter Thomas?" She stood to gather her plate and Ben's. Her nephew had jumped up from his chair, startling Royal who had been sleeping beneath the table. As if knowing the meal was over, Royal crawled out, stretched, then headed toward the main door.

"The Laramie police have not found him yet. But they'll keep trying." Joel nodded toward Royal. "Excuse me while I take him outside."

"Of course." She set the dirty dishes on the counter, then filled the sink with hot soapy water. From her position, she could watch through the window as she washed their dishes. Joel and Royal came around the corner to the clearing. Joel was saying something, likely telling Royal to get busy.

She admired him, far more than she was comfortable admitting to anyone else. If she'd thought spending more time with Joel would diminish her feelings for him, she'd been wrong. Not only was he dedicated to his search and rescue missions, but he had been nothing but patient and kind to her and Ben. And from what she could tell, his actions were genuine. Not something that he'd put on for her benefit.

Which begged the question, why wasn't he married? Or at the very least involved in a serious relationship?

None of her business, she told herself. Her job was to provide a loving home for Ben.

Tearing her gaze from the intriguing man and his dog, she scrubbed spaghetti sauce from their plates. She was just finishing the chore when Joel returned.

"Come on, Ben," Joel called as he walked into the kitchen. "We get to dry dishes."

"Why?" Ben frowned. "I'm playing my game."

"Because we don't sit around while other people do all the work." Joel's voice was firm. "Now, Ben. This won't take long."

She glanced at him. As much as she appreciated what he was doing, she was irked by the way Ben listened to him. She needed Ben to listen to her too. Yet in Joel's defense, she should have been the one to insist Ben help with the task. She was so used to taking care of everything herself it hadn't even occurred to her.

"Okay." Ben heaved a sigh, then slid off the sofa to join them.

She shot Joel a grateful look. Joel gave her a small nod, then handed Ben a dish towel and gestured to the sink. "You dry them, and I'll put them away."

Ben began to dry one of the plates. "Do you have'ta do dishes at your house?"

"Yep." Joel took the plate from him. "It's only fair

for everyone to chip in to do the work, don't you think?"

"I guess." Ben dried another plate. "But I'm just a kid."

Joel let out a snort of laughter. "So what? You have two hands, don't you? Me and my brother Justin started taking care of the horses on our ranch when we were only five years old. The rakes we used were twice as tall as we were."

Ben's eyes bugged out. "Really?"

"Really." Joel placed the dried plate in the cupboard. "And we had to take turns working in the kitchen too."

"Wow." Ben seemed impressed as he reached for a glass to dry next.

Trina swallowed the urge to tell him to be careful. What's the worst that could happen? A broken glass? She figured some losses were to be expected when leasing a property to strangers.

"Can I see your horses?" Ben asked.

"Of course." Joel caught her arched brow, and hastily added, "But only if your aunt Trina says it's okay."

"Can I, Aunt Trina?" Ben asked. "I never got to see a horse up close."

"That's fine. We'll find some time to visit the ranch before school starts." She kept the timeline vague on purpose. "But only if you behave. No more running away, okay?"

"Okay." Ben handed Joel the glass. "I promise."

Having Ben dry the dishes took twice as long, but she knew Joel was right to set an example. Until now, her focus had been on making sure Ben felt welcome in her home. That the little boy had time and space to grieve his mother's passing. Yet she understood her role as a parent was to raise Ben to be a functioning member of society.

And that included taking on responsibility. Like basic household chores. She made a mental note to do better as she drained the water from the sink.

"Can I play my video game now?" Ben asked when the last piece of silverware had been dried and put away.

Joel didn't answer, clearly leaving that one for her. *He's learning*, she thought with a wry smile. She nodded at Ben. "Yes, go ahead."

Ben tossed the dish towel aside and ran back into the living room. Royal bounded after him. She liked the way the dog had pretty much adopted Ben.

"Thanks, Joel." She glanced up at him. "I should have encouraged Ben to help with the chores."

"Hey, chipping in is part of life." Joel nodded toward Ben. "He's not too young to learn how to wash and dry dishes."

She leaned back against the counter. "As you've

proven here today. I guess I have a lot to learn about being a parent."

"Hey, you're doing fine." His smile was reassuring. "I do think keeping Ben busy is important. He might still have nightmares or dreams about his mom, that's to be expected. Yet I believe keeping him preoccupied is the best way for him to move on."

"You're right about that." It occurred to her that Ben seemed to be doing better despite not attending his counseling sessions. Not that she would pull him yet, but she had to admit Joel was right. A yawn caught her off guard, and she quickly covered her mouth with her hand. "Sorry about that. It's been a long day. I'm glad we're safe here. From the gunman," she hastily added. "Not necessarily from bears or other wild animals."

"We're fine inside the cabin. Animals won't try to get inside. I checked the clearing when I was out with Royal." He waved a hand toward the window. "And I'll do another sweep of the area before it gets too dark."

"Thanks." Maybe she should take lessons from Joel on what to watch for in the wilderness. Cody was the third biggest city in the state, but her property was very close to the hiking trail. Just because she hadn't noticed wild animals roaming too close didn't mean they weren't prone to do that.

In fact, there had been a large moose standing in the middle of the road a few months ago. She'd heard all about it when she and Ben had returned from Laramie.

"I'll go with you." She forced a smile. "You can give me my first lesson related to the local wildlife."

He grinned, and she felt the impact of his smile all the way to her toes. She tried not to frown. Joel's smile should be considered a lethal weapon, at least against women. "Great. We'll all go."

She headed into the living room and picked up her computer. It would be nice to get more writing done, but she figured finishing her scene was more than enough for now. After taking a moment to make sure she'd backed up her work and sent herself a copy via email, she logged off the device.

Stifling another yawn, she eyed Ben. The kid was fully engrossed in his new handheld video game. One concern she'd learned in her parenting books was about the negative impact of prolonged screen time on kids. Glancing at her watch, she decided to give him thirty minutes before they'd head outside.

Joel gestured to the computer. "Do you mind if we look at Robby's social media? I'm curious about his so-called friends. You can help me identify those who may know more about where he's staying."

"Sure." She carried the device to the table and opened it up. "But I'm not convinced that will help."

He shrugged. "We won't know if we don't look."

She found Robby's social media site without too much difficulty. She'd avoided looking at it after they'd broken up, not wanting to see the new woman in his life. Bad enough that Cassie from the grocery store had made a point of telling Trina all about how Robby was involved with someone else just weeks after their breakup.

As if Trina really cared.

"Who of these friends is Robby closest to?" Joel asked.

"Dean Mallory." She tapped his name on the screen.

Joel made a note of that. "Anyone else?"

She frowned, scrolling through the list of names. Finding Daisy O'Leary, she stopped. This must be Robby's current girlfriend. Daisy worked at the grocery store too. No wonder Cassie had mentioned it. "I think Daisy is his new girlfriend. Or maybe soon to be ex-girlfriend," she amended. "Daisy works at the grocery store, same as Cassie Krueger. They were both a year behind me in school."

"Okay, thanks." He wrote Daisy's name down too. "I don't know what he sees in her, though. You're prettier by far."

She felt her cheeks grow warm and knew her

fair skin was betraying her again. "Thanks, but even back in school, Daisy was known to be—well, easy." She avoided his gaze, hoping he didn't pursue the subject. "Oh, and here's Jake Rolland. He's another friend of Robby's."

After writing that name down, Joel asked, "Would Dean or Jake give Robby a place to stay if needed?"

"Absolutely." She didn't hesitate. "They've been friends since high school. Although I still think Robby was probably at his own apartment and just didn't bother to answer the door when Griff showed up."

"You could be right, but if Robby is involved in these incidents, he's likely staying away from his place. Especially since he called off sick from work." He stared at the screen for a long moment. "These names are a good place to start. Give me time to update Griff." Joel rose to his feet and reached for his phone. "When I'm finished here, we should head outside. I keep forgetting it gets darker a little earlier now."

"Sounds good." She glanced outside to see he was right about dusk beginning to fall. She closed her laptop, made sure it was plugged in to recharge the battery, then headed to the living room. "Time's up, Ben. We're going to head outside for a bit."

"No," he protested. "I wanna play."

"You'll have time to play again tomorrow." Her tone was firm. "Put it away."

Ben finally looked up at her, clearly annoyed. "You can't tell me what to do."

"Yes, I can." She suppressed a sigh. "If you want time to play tomorrow, you'll put it away now. Otherwise, I'll just take it away for the next day or two."

For a moment, he looked as if he might burst into tears. Then he threw the game aside, narrowly missing Royal.

She quickly grabbed the game. "You almost hit Royal."

Now his eyes filled with tears. He turned and buried his face against Royal's dark fur. "I'm sorry."

"What's going on?" Joel frowned as he crossed the room.

"Nothing, other than Ben has lost his video game privileges until tomorrow evening." She forced a smile. "Give me a minute to put this away and we'll be ready to go."

Joel nodded, and she quickly went into her room. She opened the bathroom drawer and tucked the video game inside.

Would parenting Ben get easier? Somehow she doubted it.

Maybe she needed to pray for God to grant her patience because she was clearly going to need it.

❧

JOEL WAITED for Ben to lift his head, tears smudging the boy's cheeks. He wasn't sure why the kid was crying, but it was time for a distraction. "We're going outside to learn about wildlife before it gets too dark."

Ben sniffled loudly. "Okay."

A few minutes later, Trina entered the room. "I'm ready." Her smile was not reflected in her deep brown eyes. Whatever had transpired over the video game still bothered her.

"Great. Let's go then. Come, Royal." His K9 didn't have to be asked twice. The dog eagerly jumped off the sofa, coming straight to his side. After a moment's hesitation, Ben came too.

He held the door for them, then led the way around to the clearing behind the cabin. "First thing, I'm going to show you what bear scat looks like."

"I can hardly wait," Trina muttered dryly.

He chuckled. "Exciting stuff, I know. But keep in mind, this is good information to learn."

"If you say so." This time, her cheeky smile was genuine.

He headed toward the opening between two trees that Ben and Royal had taken earlier. The path had clearly been used by other patrons of the cabin.

The woods grew dense, but the late western sunlight filtered through just enough to enable them to see.

He smelled the scat before he saw it, although the scent had diminished over time. Pushing aside the brush, he gestured to the pile. "This is bear scat."

"Lemme see." Ben pushed forward to peer at the mound. He frowned. "That looks like poop."

"Exactly. This is where the baby bear must have gone to the bathroom. And that's why mama grizzly grunted when you and Royal got too close."

Trina looked at the pile dubiously. "Wow, that's huge. How can you tell it's from the cub?"

"It would be much bigger if it wasn't." He shrugged. "Bear cubs grow pretty fast. A year from now, you wouldn't be able to tell whether this is from a mama or a cub."

"How do you know it's fresh?" Trina asked.

"Mostly by the smell and texture." He went on to explain what to look for. "You can tell by the dryness that this has been out for a while."

"Again, if you say so." Her tone was dubious. "For me, if I see bear scat, I'm heading back inside my house, the cabin, or any other place with walls to keep the bear far away."

"That's a good point. Ben, if you see anything resembling bear scat, you'll need to head back inside too." He held the boy's gaze. "More importantly, you need to pay attention to Royal. See how the dog isn't barking now? He was barking earlier when you came across the mama bear, right?"

Ben slowly nodded. "He was barking a lot. I didn't know why."

"Next time Royal starts to bark, pay attention. He'll always try to protect you," he explained. "And you can see he only barks for a reason."

"Okay." Ben gave a nod. "I understand."

He wanted to mention the bear's grunting sounds but decided that may be too much information at one time. "Okay, let's go a little farther. I doubt the bear is nearby, and I saw some elk droppings earlier."

"Do we need to be wary of elk too?" Trina asked as they continued along their path. "Are they protective of their young?"

"They can be, but I haven't heard of an elk attacking a human." *Not that there couldn't be a first*, he thought. "Moose are generally more likely to charge a human if the animal perceives a threat."

"Great," Trina said on a sigh. "What about bobcats?"

"They generally hunt at dusk." He pushed forward with Royal at his side until he located the elk droppings. He stopped and drew Ben closer. "What do you see there?"

"Small round poop!" Ben grinned.

"We call them elk droppings." What was it about kids who liked to say the word poop? "Deer droppings are round just like this, only slightly smaller. And as you can guess, moose droppings are bigger. Not like a bear scat, though. They're the biggest of them all."

"Big and small," Ben repeated, then he frowned. "But I only have to worry about the big smelly bear scat."

"That's right." He decided there was no point in instilling any more fear in the boy now. He hadn't come across any moose droppings on his trek around the cabin, so he felt certain they were safe from that threat source for the moment. "Okay, that's enough for one day. But you'll make sure to pay attention next time Royal barks, right? You'll know he's trying to warn you of possible danger."

"Right." Ben hopped from one foot to the other. "Because Royal is the smartest dog ever."

"Yep, he sure is." All the Sullivan K9s were smart and well trained. It was rare for any of their dogs to give a false alert. He hoped the SAR calls had slowed down a bit. He hated being out of the rotation for so long.

"Thanks for the lesson." Trina swatted at a mosquito. "Can we head back now?"

"Sure." She was so not a nature girl, and for

some reason, he found that cute. As he turned on the path, Royal suddenly went still, lifting his snout to the air and sniffing intently. He recognized that look. Something had caught the dog's attention.

He glanced around but didn't see anything alarming. "What is it, boy?"

The wind shifted just a bit. Royal sniffed for another moment, then began moving farther along the trail, his nose alternating between sniffing along the ground and scenting the air. Royal quickened his pace, another indication he was on the scent.

"What's he doing?" Trina asked in alarm. "Please tell me he's not tracking the grizzly."

"I don't think so. He's never done that before." Joel was torn between sending Trina and Ben back to the relative safety of the cabin and keeping them close. The latter won out. "Royal doesn't normally track wild game, so let's follow him for a few minutes to see what might have caught his attention."

"Okay." Trina's brown eyes were full of concern. "It can't be the gunman, though, right? He would have no way of knowing our location."

He hesitated, his gaze following Royal's progress. It seemed impossible for anyone to know where they were. Even though he didn't really think Royal was on the scent of the bear, he had never been in this sort of situation before. "I'm honestly not sure."

"That's not reassuring," Trina muttered.

He grimaced, understanding her concern. But he didn't want to lie to her about the threat level either. Royal kept moving along the path until they reached a creek. Then the dog sat and barked.

His alert? What did that mean?

"What are you telling me, Royal?" He scanned the terrain but didn't see anything remotely alarming. "Why did you bark?"

Royal simply sat there, staring up at him intently. No doubt, waiting to be rewarded with his stuffed beaver, which was back in the cabin.

After a moment, Joel slowly moved along the edge of the creek. Royal had scented something. But there wasn't a single footprint or animal print to indicate a threat.

Was he wrong about Royal tracking the bear? Maybe Royal wanted to let him know where the bear had gone since it had come so close to attacking them.

Anything was possible, although he wished there was some way to know for sure.

"What is it?" Trina asked.

"I don't know." He scanned their surroundings yet again. There hadn't been any fresh bear scat or any other animal droppings. This didn't make any sense. Royal tracked people, so maybe he should take the dog a little farther. "Let's keep going."

Trina frowned. "For how long? Ben was up early and needs to get some sleep."

"I understand, but we won't be that much longer." He bent to stroke Royal. "You're a good boy. Good boy!"

Royal jumped up, practically wiggling with joy. Then the dog put his nose to the ground and sniffed along the edge of the creek.

He didn't alert, though, which made him wonder if Royal had in fact simply tracked the bear.

"Okay, boy, heel!" He waited for Royal to wheel around, returning to his side. "Good boy." He bent to pet the dog for a moment, then straightened to look at Trina. "I'm not sure what to think. There's nothing to indicate why Royal alerted."

"What if the gunman was here?" Trina's voice was low and full of concern. "Are we safe at the cabin?"

"I'm sure we are." He spoke with a confidence he didn't entirely feel. "I'm armed, remember? And I don't think Royal alerted on the gunman. If so, he'd continue following the scent. Maybe he had scented the bear and knew the animal posed a danger to us."

"Okay." She didn't look reassured. Hard to blame her.

"Let's go, Royal." He didn't reward his K9 for the alert, mostly because he had no idea what Royal was trying to tell him. Times like this he really wished Royal could talk.

"Come, Ben," Trina called. "Time to head back."

Ben didn't argue but kept his stick in hand as they followed the path back to the cabin. As they walked, Joel's mind whirled.

Why had Royal alerted? Were they really safe at the cabin?

He honestly didn't know.

10

Trina was not thrilled with the idea of sharing the woods around their rental cabin with a bear. Especially a mama who'd already almost attacked Ben to protect her cub. It wasn't that she didn't trust Joel to protect them, she did. When they'd first arrived at the cabin, it had been a relief to feel safe. The two shooting incidents, the fire, then having to leave the hotel only be under fire for a third time had been more than anyone should have to handle.

The cabin had represented a bit of normalcy, well, as much as possible while spending time with Joel under the same roof. Yet now that secure feeling had abruptly dissipated, replaced by the nagging feeling of being in danger. As they walked through the woods, she couldn't help glancing frequently over her shoulder, expecting someone or something to pounce on them at any moment.

She shivered as the temperature cooled with the setting sun. Maybe it was her imagination running amok, but she saw a couple of shadows beyond the trees.

Stop it! Don't let fear rule your life, she silently lectured herself. *It's not healthy, especially for Ben.*

As they retraced their steps toward the cabin, Royal ran ahead sniffing the ground with interest. If the K9 was worried about the shadows, he didn't show it. She tried to relax, knowing Royal would let them know of a threat. Human or animal.

The way he'd alerted at the creek? She grimaced. Seeing Royal alert there had been creepy, and despite Joel's nonchalant comments to the contrary, she could tell he'd been bothered by the dog's alert too.

She wanted to weep with relief when the cabin came into view.

"Go inside." Joel gestured to the clearing along the front of the structure. "I'm going to give Royal time to get busy."

"Sounds good." She opened the door, turning to glance down at Ben. "Time to get ready for bed."

"Aw, Auntie Trina, do I have'ta? I don't wanna go

to bed." Ben's whiny voice only reinforced how tired he really was. And on cue, the boy yawned. Then he asked, "Can I play my game for a while?"

"Not tonight." She leveled him with a hard look as she held the door for him. "You threw the video game and almost hit Royal, remember? You don't get the game back until tomorrow evening."

"That long?" His lower lip trembled.

"We'll see." She suppressed a sigh. Being wishy-washy wasn't smart. "Now go in to brush your teeth and wash your face."

"Okay." Ben walked in slow motion as if he couldn't bear the thought of going to bed. Why kids fought against sleeping, she had no idea. She wished now that she'd set a different timeline for him to regain his video privileges. Why was it that punishing a child ended up punishing the parent more than the kid?

Kids needed to come with a training manual. One that explained exactly how to help a child understand there are consequences for their actions. Maybe when this was over, she'd check out the library to find more parenting books. There was so much she still needed to learn to become the best guardian possible for Ben.

She'd already made some mistakes. From here, she could only hope that she didn't mess up too badly.

Listening at the bathroom door, Trina was grateful to hear water running in the bathroom. At least Ben was doing what he'd been told for once.

Covering her mouth as she yawned, she glanced out the window at Joel and Royal. They were standing in the front of the cabin, Joel watching his K9 with a serious gaze. She wasn't sure what they were doing, until the dog lowered his nose to the ground and began to sniff the grass around the SUV.

She frowned. Had Royal alerted again?

"Auntie Trina, I'm done," Ben called.

"Coming." She turned away from the window, hurrying into Ben's room. He was wearing his favorite race-car pajamas. "Get under the covers."

"But I'm not sleepy." He opened his brown eyes wide, as if to prove his point. "Will you tell me a story?"

"Yes, I'll tell you a story." She'd been making up a story for Ben each night, using him as the main character. She didn't write books for kids and was basically winging it each night, but so far Ben hadn't complained about her lame stories. "Once upon a time, there was a boy named Ben who could talk to the animals in the forest."

"Like the mama grizzly?" Ben asked, his eyelids already starting to droop.

"Yes, exactly. Ben was walking through the

woods one day when he saw the big scary-looking mama bear. He wasn't afraid because he knew she was just trying to protect her baby. When the mama bear growled and roared loudly, Ben lifted his hand and told her not to be worried because he would never ever hurt her cub."

Ben forced his drooping eyelids open. "Then what happened?"

"Well, the mama bear could speak the same special language as young Ben. She tipped her large head to the side, looking at him for a long time. Until that moment, mama bear hadn't realized she could talk to little boys too. She nodded her large head, understanding at last that Ben would not hurt her baby. She said thank you for being kind, then turned and walked away." She hid a smile as Ben's eyes slid the rest of the way closed. "And from that day forward, Ben told all the animals he met in the forest they were safe from him. Especially the mama animals with babies standing beside them. The end."

Moving cautiously, she stood and made her way to the bedroom door. Ben didn't stir as she switched the overhead light off. The rooms each had a small nightlight, which she left glowing in case Ben needed to use the bathroom. Then she tiptoed down the hall to the main living space.

Joel and Royal were still outside. She watched through the window for another moment, then turned away. Obviously, Joel could take care of his K9 without her help. Deciding there was nothing to be alarmed about, she turned and headed into her room.

Ben wasn't the only one who was exhausted. She was well into her last bit of reserves. It seemed as if she'd run a full marathon from the moment she'd woken up only to discover Ben had gone missing, until now. She quickly changed into her sleep shorts and sleep shirt, then crawled into bed.

Despite her bone-weary fatigue, she didn't immediately fall asleep. Her mind replayed the series of events throughout the day, ending with Royal's unexpected and unexplained alert near the creek.

She must have fallen asleep at some point because Joel's hand on her shoulder had her bolting upright in bed. "What's wrong?"

"I think we need to get out of here." Joel's low, grim tone filled her with dread.

"Why?" She pushed her hair from her eyes. "What changed? Did Royal alert on the gunman's scent?"

"I'm still not sure what caught Royal's attention. I had him check the area around the cabin and our SUV, and he didn't alert here, so the creek could be a false alarm." He paused, then added, "It's bothering me that Royal doesn't normally alert on animal scents. And he doesn't make many mistakes either. I promised to keep you and Ben safe, so that means taking extra precautions. I'll feel terrible if something bad happens because we stayed."

"What time is it?" She had no idea how long she'd been asleep. "I don't really want to wake Ben unless we absolutely have to. He needs his sleep."

"It's ten thirty." Now that her eyes were adjusting to the dim light, she could see the indecision in Joel's gaze. "What if I'm wrong about why Royal alerted at the creek?"

"He's smart, Joel, but he's still a dog, right? Nobody is perfect. Besides, we've only been asleep for ninety minutes." She tried to hide her annoyance "If Royal hasn't alerted anywhere around the cabin, then my vote is to stay here. Besides, where would we go? We're not likely to get a hotel room at this hour."

"I have camping gear—a tent, sleeping bag, and other stuff in the SUV."

Camping? In the dark? In the woods where they'd run across a bear just a few hours ago? Was he joking? She stared at him. "No way. Uh-uh. Not happening."

"Then we'll sleep in the car. The front seats recline, and Ben can stretch out on the back seat."

His persistence was frustrating. "I don't see why that's necessary. You've said from the very beginning that Royal will let us know if there's a problem. And I believe the dog was warning us about the bear at the creek, and that he'll bark or growl if he catches the gunman's scent." She yawned and lay back down on the bed. Ben wasn't the only one who needed sleep. She didn't have the energy for this. She closed her eyes and turned onto her side so that she wasn't facing him. "Good night, Joel."

He lingered for a few more seconds, but then she heard a soft, "Good night."

She sighed, relaxing her muscles. This was better than camping in a tent or sleeping in the car. Less than a few minutes later, she was sound asleep.

A crying sound penetrated her consciousness. Pushing herself upright, she quickly realized Ben was crying. She jumped out of bed and hurried to the room next door.

"Shh, Ben, it's okay. You're fine." She sat on the edge of the bed and pulled the little boy into her arms, wishing there was something she could do to help ease his grief over losing his mother. "It's okay. I'm here."

"I talked to the mama bear, but she didn't listen." He sobbed against her shoulder. "She kept roaring and slashing at me with her paws. Then she said she was gonna eat me for dinner!"

"Oh, Ben, I'm sorry." She probably shouldn't have made up that bedtime story about the bear. See? That was why she needed an owner's manual on raising kids! How was she to know her attempt to spin a tale would end like this? "Don't worry, you're safe now. That was just a bad dream. The mama bear and her cub are far away."

He cried for another minute before his sobs began to fade away. He sniffled loudly and wiped his face against her sleep shirt. "I would never hurt the mama's baby bear."

"Oh, Ben, of course you wouldn't." She tried to think of a way to reassure him. "Maybe you and Royal startled her, and that's why she was so scared of you."

Ben lifted his head. "She was scared of me?"

"Yes. I think all wild animals are afraid of humans." Was that true? She hoped she wasn't lying, but she pressed on. "She was scared, so she went up on her hind legs to make herself look bigger to scare you away from her baby."

"Oh, I see." Realization dawned. "That's why Joel waved his arms and shouted back at her."

"Yep, you and Joel were scared, but so was the mama bear. But in the end, she realized you wouldn't hurt her and left you alone. All she really cares about is that her cub is safe." She hugged him again. "Just like all I want is for you to be safe."

Ben rested against her. "I get it now."

"Good." She brushed his damp hair from his forehead. "It's still dark outside, so you need to go back to sleep."

"Okay." To her surprise, he hugged her, then snuggled back down into the covers. "Good night, Auntie Trina."

"Good night, Ben." She pressed a kiss to the top of his head, then rose and crossed to the doorway. Pausing, she looked back at him, her heart aching for what he was going through. Losing his mother, moving to Cody, now hiding in a cabin in the woods.

And her bright idea of a bedtime story hadn't helped. She needed to read more children's books to understand what types of stories kids Ben's age liked to read. Nothing scary from this point on.

"Everything okay?" Joel's voice coming from the end of the hallway almost made her scream. She put a hand over her pounding heart and managed a nod.

"Fine. Ben had a bad dream." She tugged on the hem of her sleep shirt, feeling self-conscious. "Sorry to wake you."

"You didn't. I haven't been sleeping much." His dry tone made her wince.

And that was her fault? Because she hadn't wanted to go on a camping adventure in the middle of the night? "Sorry about that. Good night." She quickly ducked into her room and closed the door.

As Trina struggled to fall back asleep, she realized most women wouldn't have minded camping in the woods with Joel, even knowing a grizzly had been in the area. Joel deserved to have someone to do those spontaneous things with him. She had no doubt his sisters were the same way. Ready, willing, and able to do whatever was necessary under the circumstances.

It hurt to know she and Joel were completely wrong for each other.

AFTER TRINA WENT BACK to bed, Joel continued prowling around the kitchen. Royal looked at him from the sofa as if trying to understand what the problem was.

"Your alert is my problem," he whispered.

Royal cocked his head to the side as if asking why.

With a sigh, he turned away. Now that he was awake, again, he peered through the windows, checking the yard again, the way he had several times during the night. He hadn't seen anything alarming.

And of course, Royal had slept like a baby. His K9 snored, which was both cute and annoying.

Especially when Joel wasn't getting any sleep.

Okay, to be fair, he'd managed almost four hours. Not consecutive hours by any stretch of the imagination, but still better than nothing. Royal closed his eyes and fell asleep again. Shaking his head, Joel stifled a yawn and glanced for the zillionth time at his watch. Six o'clock was well past coffee time.

Trying to be as quiet as possible, he filled the carafe with water and added the coffee grounds. He leaned against the counter waiting for the coffee to brew while watching Royal. His K9 showed no interest in going out to get busy, probably because Joel had let the dog outside at midnight.

He wondered about Ben's nightmare. Hearing the boy's sobs, he'd been about to head down the hall to talk to him, but Trina had beat him to it. Which really was probably for the best. Things were difficult for them, but he knew it wouldn't take Ben long to see Trina as his mother. Memories of his loss would fade over time, and Trina would be the constant presence in his life.

Yet getting there would still be a rocky road for Trina and Ben to travel. What had upset Ben this time? Another bad dream related to his mother's passing?

Poor kid, he hated to see the boy suffer.

When the coffee finished, he poured a large mug and padded back into the living room. Anticipating Royal would need to go outside sooner or later, he set his coffee aside to slip his boots on and lace them up.

Royal didn't move.

"Glad one of us is getting some shut-eye," he whispered dryly. He scrubbed his hands over his face, then reached for his coffee. Normally, this was his favorite time of the day. But he was still too tired and cranky to appreciate it.

A moment later, he heard a door open. Trina came into the kitchen wearing clean clothes.

"Who can resist coffee?" She shot him a quick glance as she reached for a cup. "Thanks for making it for me. I'm sorry if we kept you up last night."

"You didn't." As the early rays of morning sunlight began to creep over the horizon, he realized his fears were unwarranted. He'd stayed up until well past midnight for no good reason. Well, Royal's alert wasn't nothing, but his K9 must have scented something else. Either the bear or some other creature that his K9 wanted to warn him about. "I'm the one who woke you."

"It's fine." She filled her cup and carried it to the kitchen table. "I'm glad everything was quiet last night, well, except for Ben's nightmare."

"His mother?" Joel stood and joined her at the table.

She winced. "No, I told him a bedtime story about a boy with special powers who can talk to animals, like the mama grizzly bear. Turns out, he had a nightmare that the bear didn't listen to him and tried to eat him."

"Yikes." He cocked his head. "You made up that story on the fly?"

"Yeah, which was the problem. I should have realized he didn't need to be reminded of his close encounter with the grizzly."

"Hey, he may have had that nightmare regardless." He reached over to pat her hand. "Don't beat yourself up. I think a story about a boy who can talk to animals is a great idea."

"You're an adult. He's eight." She shook her head. "That's my whole problem. I don't have enough exposure to kids his age to know what will hold his interest versus scaring him to death."

"I wish I could help, but my memories of being eight are somewhat vague." He hid a smile behind his mug. "And considering how much our older siblings teased us, I doubt we'd be afraid of the same things as Ben."

She frowned. "You're accusing me of being overprotective?"

"No, but I am pointing out that my childhood

was very different. Our parents were working the ranch and didn't have a lot of time to pay attention to their nine kids." He waved a hand. "I'm not complaining, just stating a fact."

"Well, that's easy for you to say. I'm doing my best." She sounded cranky, and he had to resist the urge to draw her into his arms.

Enough. He couldn't afford to think about Trina as anything more than a friend. Time to stay focused on the very real threat of danger. He needed an update from Griff soon. The Laramie PD should know where Peter Thomas is by now. And he wanted to know if the video outside the Lumberjack Inn had revealed anything of interest. Finally, he wanted to know where Robby Rawlings was.

But for now, they needed to eat. He stood and moved toward the counter. "I'll start breakfast."

"I can help." The words were no sooner out of her mouth when Ben's bedroom door opened.

"Aunt Trina? Where's Royal?" The boy came into the kitchen, his feet bare and his reddish hair adorably mussed.

"Royal's sleeping." Joel nodded to the sofa.

"Let's get you showered and dressed, okay?" Trina rose. "I'm sure Royal will be awake once you're finished."

"Okay." Joel was amazed the kid didn't argue. Maybe Trina was right that he'd needed some sleep.

His experience with Eli, Chase and Wynona's son, was limited. And really, Eli was so quiet it wasn't a fair comparison.

Remembering Ben's favorite breakfast food was scrambled eggs, he set about making a large batch. In another skillet, he fried bacon.

Royal slid off the sofa, stretched, then padded into the kitchen. Joel eyed his K9 who sniffed the air with interest.

"Are you begging?"

Instantly, Royal looked away as if caught in the act, then wandered over to his water dish. The trainer Maya had hired for their dogs had made a big deal out of telling the K9s in a firm tone *no begging*. The dogs were programmed to ignore table food, even to the point of recognizing the phrase.

"Good boy." He eyed the clock. "You'll get your breakfast soon. Let's wait until Ben is ready."

Ben and Trina returned to the kitchen just as breakfast was ready. "Have a seat." Joel waved at the table, which was set and full of food. "I need to feed Royal, then I'll join you."

"We'll wait, since we need to say grace." Trina arched a brow when Ben tried to steal a slice of bacon. "Wait, Ben."

Joel filled Royal's bowl, gave the dog permission to eat, then quickly dropped into his seat. He bowed his head. "Dear Lord Jesus, we thank You for this food we are blessed to eat. We ask that You continue to keep us safe in Your care. And please provide the police the wisdom and bravery to find the person responsible. Amen."

"Amen," Trina said.

A half beat later, Ben chimed in too. "Amen." He chomped a piece of bacon, then asked, "Why can't the police say their own prayers?"

"They can. But we can all pray for each other, right?" He glanced at Trina, who nodded encouragingly. "I pray for my brothers and sisters, just like they probably pray for me."

"So we should pray for each other? Kinda like giving presents on birthdays?" Ben asked.

"Ben, it's not polite to hint for a birthday present." Trina rolled her eyes. "Your birthday was in March. You have a long way to go until your next one."

Ben sighed. "March is really far away."

Joel knew better than to make any promises he might not be able to keep. March was a long way off, and his immediate concern was making sure Trina and Ben were able to return home safely.

"Eat your eggs." Trina spread jelly on a piece of toast and handed that to Ben. "You have to finish up if you want to play with Royal."

"Okay." Ben took a big bite of his toast. "Why didn't we get more Pop-Tarts? I like those better."

"Those are only for a special treat." Trina's patience was admirable.

They finished their meal a few minutes later. Trina got up first, carrying her dirty plate and Joel's to the sink. "I'll do the dishes," she offered. "You cooked."

"That's fine." Royal looked up at him, then walked to the front door. That was his cue that he needed to go outside. "Do you have to go outside, boy? Do you?"

"Can I come too?" Ben asked.

Joel nodded. "Sure, but we need to give Royal time to get busy, okay? After that, you can play."

"Okay!" Ben slid off his chair.

"Hold on," Joel held up a hand. "Carry your dirty dishes to the sink."

Ben hesitated, then reached for the plate. He carried it to the sink, where Trina thanked him.

"Behave," she warned as Joel opened the front door for Royal.

The dog hurried over to do his thing. Then he lifted his nose to the air, sniffing intently. Joel hoped his K9 wasn't about to make another false alert.

Royal darted toward the SUV, sniffing the ground near the tires. Then he let out a sharp bark.

Instantly, Joel swept Ben up into his arms and hurried up to the house. He opened the door and set Ben inside. Royal came inside, too, which he found odd. He'd intended to make another sweep of the area without Ben being anywhere close.

"Trina, Royal alerted—" His voice broke when a loud explosion rocked the earth. Knocked off his feet, Joel hit the floor and rolled halfway across the kitchen floor, coming up hard against the edge of the counter. Stunned, he glanced over his shoulder.

And saw the SUV was a ball of fire.

<h1 style="text-align:center">11</h1>

The explosion knocked Trina to the floor. Ben cried out in alarm as he, too, fell to the floor. She frantically crawled toward Ben, her ears ringing. Reaching her nephew, she drew him close, trying to ascertain if he was hurt.

He was crying, but it took her a moment to realize she couldn't hear him. "It's okay, Ben," she shouted, despite knowing he probably couldn't hear anything either. "I'm here! It's okay!"

Strong hands gripped her shoulders. She lifted her gaze to see Joel standing over her. His lips were moving, and he gestured toward the back door of the cabin. Understanding he wanted her to get out of there, she pushed herself upright. Ben was too heavy for her, but she pulled on his arm to let him know he needed to stand.

Then Joel bent and hauled the boy into his arms. He snagged a large backpack from the side of the counter and headed for the back door. She was tempted to grab her computer but didn't. Thankfully, she always emailed a copy of her book to herself, so she wouldn't lose her current work in progress.

The other files on her laptop were another story. But there was no time to worry about them now. She staggered after Joel and Ben. Royal stayed close to Joel's side.

Outside, the air was thick with acrid smoke. Much like when her house had been set on fire. She glanced back over her shoulder, seeing dark plumes of smoke rising above the cabin.

She could hardly believe a bomb had been set near the cabin. Reeling from shock and horror, she followed Joel, Ben, and Royal into the woods. For a brief moment, she thought about the mama grizzly, then forced the panic away. They had bigger things to worry about.

Like whether the bomber was waiting for them in the foliage, intending to finish them off for good.

Why was this happening? How had the gunman found them there?

She tripped over a fallen limb, barely managing to stay upright. Questions that had no answers could wait, this was the time to pay attention. Joel glanced back at her, clearly impatient with their lack of progress. Putting on a burst of speed, she quickly caught up to him.

Her ears were still ringing from the blast, and she had no idea how long that would last. Her gaze dropped to Royal who was sniffing the ground intently. Had Joel given him the search command? The last thing she wanted was for the three of them to walk straight toward the gunman.

Joel continued to push forward, the backpack dangling from one arm, as he held Ben. Her nephew rested his head on Joel's shoulder, and she was deeply grateful for Joel's strength and determination to keep them safe.

After twenty minutes of walking, Joel came to a stop near a fallen tree. He bent to set Ben on the ground, then turned to look at her. "Are you hurt?"

Grateful she could hear, she shook her head. "I'm fine. But what happened?"

His grim expression was hard. "Royal alerted near the SUV. I grabbed Ben and came inside the house just to be on the safe side, then the car exploded."

She stared at him. "How did he find us?"

"I don't know, but we need to keep moving." He turned to Ben. "Can you walk on your own?"

The boy nodded, wiping tears from his face. "I'm scared."

Her heart broke for him. Ben didn't deserve this. None of them did, but he was the true innocent victim in this nightmare.

"Hey, I'm going to do everything possible to keep you safe, okay?" Joel held Ben's gaze. "Royal will let us know if there's a reason to be afraid. The sooner we get away from the cabin, though, the better. That means I need you to follow my lead, okay?"

"Okay." Ben sniffled loudly.

Joel glanced at her, and she nodded as well. "Don't worry, we'll keep up."

"Good." He took a minute to shoulder his pack, then stepped forward. "Stay close."

"Go ahead, Ben." She nudged the boy in the back, urging him to follow Joel. "I'll be right behind you."

Ben didn't argue, seeming to understand the seriousness of their situation. She was both glad for the fact that he was going along with the plan and concerned about how the little boy would ever bounce back from this. As if the gunfire and house fire weren't enough. Now they were heading into the woods where the mama grizzly may not be too far away.

She fell into step behind Ben to better protect him. Royal had moved ahead of Joel, his nose either sweeping the ground or sniffing the air around them. Reassured, she tried to relax her tense shoulders.

They walked for what seemed like forever. Mosquitos and gnats buzzed around her. She swatted at them half-heartedly. Joel and Royal took them up an incline, making her groan under her breath. Her thigh muscles burned as she strove to keep up as promised. Her attempts to hike the trail near her home were pathetically laughable compared to what she'd been through the past twenty-four hours.

She really needed to get in better shape. Not that she ever wanted to be in danger like this again.

When they reached a rocky outcropping, Joel stopped and shrugged out of his pack. Grateful for the opportunity to rest, she sat on the edge of the rock, brushing her hot sweaty hair away from her face.

"I don't have a lot of water." Joel sounded apologetic as he rummaged through his pack. He pulled a water bottle out and passed it to her. "You can have a sip and so can Ben. I need to save some for Royal."

"I understand." She took a sip and passed it to Ben. "Only a little bit, okay?"

"I know." Ben took a small sip from the bottle, then handed it to Joel. "Thank you." His tone was subdued. Her heart ached over the lingering fear in Ben's brown eyes.

She couldn't help glancing up at the partly cloudy sky above the trees. She opened her heart and begged God to keep Ben safe. To heal his wounds, especially his grief over losing his mother.

Surprisingly, she felt better after the prayer. Maybe Joel was onto something. Hopefully, she'd be able to learn more about God and faith when this nightmare was over.

"We'll have more water if we can find that creek again." Joel's comment interrupted her thoughts. He took a sip of water, then poured some into a collapsible bowl for Royal. The black lab lapped at the water, then looked up at Joel as if waiting for his next command.

"Take a break, Royal." Joel slid the water bottle in a zippered pocket. Seeing the backpack up close, she realized it was huge. Hadn't Joel mentioned having a tent and a sleeping bag? Hard to imagine all of that stuffed inside, but then again, she was certain Joel was more than prepared for anything they might face.

Including the gunman? Yes, she decided. Especially him.

Joel pulled out his phone, stared at the screen for a moment, then tucked it away. At her questioning look, he shook his head. "No service here. We must be far enough away from the cabin that we can't get a signal. I'll try in a while with my satellite phone. For now, I'd rather keep moving, just in case."

She swallowed hard and nodded. She understood what he was saying. Moving forward was the best way to avoid the gunman following them. She'd trust his judgment on this.

If anyone could keep her and Ben safe, it was Joel and Royal.

And they had God on their side.

JOEL WAS KICKING himself ten ways to Sunday for his failure to take Royal's alert last night at the creek bed seriously. What had Maya's trainer repeated over and over again?

Trust your dog. Always, always trust your dog.

Well Joel hadn't done that, and if not for Royal's keen nose alerting them mere seconds before the explosion, his lapse in judgment would have gotten them all killed.

He couldn't afford to make a mistake like that again.

Swallowing hard, he checked his compass and GPS coordinates. By his estimation, they'd come across the creek at a higher altitude if he continued along these coordinates. He'd decided to head in the opposite direction from yesterday for two reasons.

He wanted to be sure he avoided the area where the gunman had been yesterday and to avoid the mama grizzly. Not that he could guarantee his strategy would work on either count.

Grizzlies roamed for miles, especially around fresh water where they could find an adequate supply of fish. They preferred salmon, but trout would do just as well. Along with the assortment of wild berries.

Worse than that, though, he had no idea where the gunman had been last night. Royal had alerted near the creek but hadn't caught the scent heading back to the cabin. Maybe the gunman had walked for a while in the creek to throw off the scent. As it had been cooler last night, the gunman may not have sweated enough to provide an additional scent source either.

But then where had the guy been? He'd taken Royal out last night before bed, using his K9 to clear the entire area. Royal hadn't alerted once.

The most likely scenario was that the gunman had camped a good couple of miles upwind of the creek where Royal alerted. From that point, the gunman could have waited until the dead of night to approach the cabin and to plant the bomb beneath the SUV. Royal hadn't raised the alarm, but the dog had been wiped out from the long trek. He didn't blame his K9 for Joel's mistake.

Had the guy watched through binoculars, waiting for the opportunity to trigger the explosive? Or had the device been put on a timer of some sort? He hadn't taken Royal out as early as he normally did because the dog hadn't needed to go out.

A chill snaked down his spine by what may have happened if he'd taken Royal out earlier. When the dog alerted, he'd have gotten Ben and Trina out of the cabin and into the SUV, heading back toward Cody.

If the device had indeed been on a timer, they'd have died in the explosion.

Blowing out a breath, he turned to scan their surroundings. Imagining the worst-case scenario wasn't helpful. He needed to be alert for any sign of this guy being nearby. The other reason he'd chosen this particular route was because the wind was coming out of the southeast. If the guy tried to follow them through the woods, Royal should easily catch his scent in time to warn them.

Yet the way the gunman had been one step ahead of them from the very beginning ticked him off, big time. He could not underestimate this guy again.

So much for promising to keep Trina and Ben safe. He'd barely managed to help them escape certain death.

Shaking off the depressing thought, he turned to

check on Trina and Ben. Royal was stretched out beneath the shadow of the rock, not showing any sign of concern.

He bent to scratch the dog behind his silky ears. "You're going to find that gunman before he finds us, right, boy?"

Royal's tail swished back and forth across the ground in agreement.

He straightened and shouldered the pack. "Time for us to go."

"Okay." Trina looked tired but didn't complain. She stood and smiled down at her nephew. "Are you ready, Ben?"

"Yep." In contrast to Trina's wan expression, Ben looked raring to go. Apparently, getting a good night's sleep had helped Ben.

That still wasn't an excuse to ignore Royal's alert.

"I need you to alert us to danger," he told Royal in a low voice. "Either from the bad guy or the bear, I need you to help me, okay?"

Royal lifted his snout and took in the various scents. After a moment, the dog moved forward. Joel rested his hand on the butt of his weapon, setting an easy pace for Ben and Trina's sake.

They walked in silence for several minutes. Birds chirped and the sky beyond the towering tree branches lightened as the sun rose. The temperature would soon get hot, but under these circumstances, that was better than being in a blizzard.

He wished again that he'd asked Justin to stay with them at the cabin. So what if that meant taking them out of the search and rescue rotation? Trina and Ben's safety was more important than strangers who got lost in the woods.

"Auntie Trina, did you remember to bring my video game?" Ben asked a few minutes later.

"I'm afraid not." She shot him a look of remorse. "But don't forget we still have your original game at my house. I'm sure we'll be able to get that sometime soon."

"Okay." For once, Ben didn't whine or argue about the game. "Let's play I spy with my little eye."

Trina hesitated, glancing at him as if asking permission. Voices could carry in the woods, but he was trusting Royal to alert them to danger. And maybe talking would keep the wild animals at bay. He nodded. "That's fine."

"Okay, Ben. I spy with my little eye something blue."

"That's easy, there's a bluebird sitting up in the tree." Ben grinned as if he'd won the lottery. "I spy with my little eye something red."

Joel tuned out the game, keeping his concentration on the path before them and on Royal. His K9 was doing a good job of sniffing the ground as they walked. By Joel's estimation, they'd reach the creek in another twenty minutes. There they could take a break and enjoy some fresh water.

Thank goodness they'd already eaten breakfast. He had granola bars but hoped to hold off on those for a while. At least until lunchtime. If Ben could last that long.

He had his satellite phone and hoped to reach his family soon. Although even then, he wasn't sure how long it would take them to get there. Especially since he didn't intend to stay in one place for long.

Keeping an eye on his watch, he decided to keep going for a while longer. Best to be far from the cabin before making the call.

He lifted his gaze to the sky and silently begged God for strength and wisdom to keep Trina and Ben safe.

His prayer didn't instill the level of confidence he'd hoped for, but he reminded himself he needed to do his part in this. God would come through for them when they needed Him the most. With that, Joel concentrated on pushing forward. Reaching the creek would help. First, they needed fresh water. Then he'd call his family. When he had a timeline for their potential rescue, he'd think about their next meal.

Maybe rainbow trout. He had a fishing line with him, along with a fishing license. Although if he ran across a game warden, he'd be thankful for the escort out of there.

He heard the creek before he saw it. Following Royal's lead, he used his forearm to push the tree branches aside.

The creek water ran at a brisk pace. Royal bent his head to drink. He turned back to see Ben and Trina lagging a little behind.

"Break time." He smiled. "We have fresh water."

"I'm really thirsty," Ben said, jumping over a fallen branch to join him. "Look at Royal! Can I drink like that?"

"Go ahead." He and Justin had done that plenty. The creek water wouldn't hurt them; its source was snow melting from the highest part of the mountain.

Ben dropped to his stomach beside Royal and used his hands to drink.

Trina joined him a moment later. Without a word, she did exactly as Ben, stretching out on the ground and drinking deeply from her cupped hands. Then she stuck her face in the water, staying submerged for a solid thirty seconds before lifting her head and swiping water from her eyes.

"Feels so good." She sighed. "I never thought I'd be so happy to see a creek."

Joel smiled faintly as he shrugged out of his pack, then took a turn at the creek. The water felt amazing against his hot skin, but he didn't linger. He filled the water bottle with water, then rose to his feet.

Carrying the bottle to the pack, he set it aside until he'd found the sat phone. He made room for the water bottle, then stood with the bag. Scanning their surroundings, he gestured to the clearing that was on the opposite side of the creek. "See that spot over there? I'm going to head there to make the call, the trees are too thick here. I'd like you to stay here with Ben and Royal."

"Okay." Trina sat with her back pressed against a tree trunk. Ben splashed Royal, and the dog responded by shaking himself to get rid of the excess water from his coat.

He found a spot to cross the water, using a rock as a stepping stone. In the clearing, he pulled out his sat phone and searched for a connection.

It took a minute for the device to find the closest satellite. When the signal finally connected, a wave of relief hit hard.

"Sullivan K9 Search and Rescue," Anna's cheerful tone filled his ears.

"Anna, it's Joel. Is Justin or Trevor around? I need help, and fast."

"Justin is here, but Trevor and Kendra are out on a call." Anna's tone turned serious. "What do you need?"

He hesitated, unwilling to tell her the gruesome details about the SUV being bombed. "We need a ride. Let me talk to Justin, okay?"

"Of course. Hold please." He imagined Anna using her cell phone to let Justin know to pick up the landline.

Thirty seconds later, he heard Justin's voice. "Joel? What happened? I've had a bad feeling about you all morning. Especially after I left you several messages without hearing back from you until now."

Justin often claimed to have twin telepathy, and sometimes that was true. Joel had experienced the same sense of dread right before Justin was in trouble. "We were found at the cabin, not sure how. Royal alerted near a creek late last night. It didn't seem possible he'd picked up the gunman's scent, but he did. Sometime during the night, the guy planted a bomb beneath the SUV. It exploded, but we were able to get away."

"A bomb?" Justin's voice rose in alarm. "That's crazy!"

"Tell me about it." Joel continued scanning the area as they talked. "I'm going to send you my current coordinates, but I don't feel safe sticking around for long. We need to keep moving."

"Understood. Send them to me," Justin said. "I'll head out ASAP to meet you."

"Thanks, bro." He read off his GPS coordinates, then said, "I know it's going to take you forty minutes just to reach Cody, not to mention heading even farther north. I was thinking we should turn around to make our way back down the mountain. I came this way so we'd be far enough from the cabin to avoid running into him."

"Maybe you should wait on that," Justin advised. "I've pulled up your coordinates, and there's a small campground less than three miles due west from your current location." Justin read off those coordinates. "I'll meet you there."

He hadn't known about the campground, although the mountains were full of such places. Memorizing the location, he put his GPS and compass away. "That sounds good. But, Justin, ask Anna to pack lunch. We're going to be hungry."

"Will do. But keep your eyes open, bro. I don't trust this guy not to find a way to track you down."

"Trust me, I've been concerned about the same thing." He had to assume the gunman had somehow tracked Trina's internet connection to the cabin. It was the only option that made sense. That wouldn't be a problem now, so they had that much going for them. Yet he also knew the gunman might anticipate they'd head to the campground.

If he knew about it.

Either way, Joel would approach the campsite

with caution, using Royal to scout the area for them prior to getting too close. "We'll be fine. The good news is that Royal knows this guy's scent."

"Always helpful to have a solid K9 on board. Stay safe, Joel." Justin paused, then added, "Anna is packing lunch for you now, and I'll be on the road in ten."

"Thanks. See you soon." Joel disconnected the sat phone connection. Help was on the way, but they weren't out of danger yet. Three miles with a woman who didn't especially enjoy the outdoors and an eight-year-old would not be a piece of cake.

He quickly crossed back to the other side of the creek. "Are you ready to keep going?"

A flash of disappointment darkened Trina's gaze, but she quickly nodded. "Sure. We're ready, right, Ben?"

"I guess so. But how much farther do we have to go?" Ben's face turned pouty, showing the first signs of his being tired of the hike.

Joel didn't dare mention the three miles they had to cover, which would seem like a lifetime to Ben. And likely to Trina too. "Not too far. My brother Justin is going to meet up with us very soon."

"Oh yeah?" That cheered Ben. "He'll have a car, right?"

"Right." He shouldered the backpack. "Come, Royal."

His K9 stood, stretched, then trotted after him. Joel set out following the most direct path possible to the campground. Trina fell behind Ben in their usual formation.

"I'm hungry," Ben complained.

"I have granola bars here." He had put them in the side pocket, anticipating this. He pulled one free and handed it to Ben. Then he stretched out to give Trina the second one. "This should hold you over until we meet Justin. He's bringing lunch."

"That's nice of him," Trina said with a smile.

"Nice of Anna," Joel corrected. "She's the glue that holds our ranch together."

Ben was quiet as he ate his snack. Joel pushed their pace as much as possible. Now that he had a destination in mind, he was anxious to get there.

Hopefully before the gunman.

They walked for fifteen minutes straight, before Trina called out, "Joel, I can't go that fast."

He stopped and turned to see she and Ben were lagging behind. "Sorry about that."

"Where are we meeting your brother?" Trina asked after a few minutes. "I don't see anything but trees."

"There's a campground close by." He forced a smile. "We can eat lunch there if you'd like."

She glanced down at Ben, who'd found another stick. "If Ben's hungry, we'll eat if that's okay."

"No problem." He wished there was a way to make this hike through the woods easier for them.

Joel checked their coordinates often, and when they were within a quarter mile of the campground, he stopped. "Hold on for a minute."

Trina looked happy to stop, as did Ben. He bent near Royal. "Search, boy. Search bad guy."

Royal sniffed the air. The wind had shifted a bit so that if the gunman was nearby, Royal should be able to alert on his scent.

"Why is he searching the bad guy?" Alarm tinged Trina's voice.

"I just want to be sure he's not around. Stay back near the trees with Ben, okay?" Joel moved forward as Royal began his usual zigzag pattern.

This was one time he prayed his K9 would not alert.

12

———————

Trina put her arm around Ben, pulling him close as she watched Joel and Royal work. She glanced around, her nerves stretched razor thin. First the explosion and now a long hike through the woods, and they still weren't safe.

She wondered if this nightmare would ever end.

"What's going on?" Ben frowned up at her. He still held his stick and whacked it against the tree a few times. "Why are we just standing here?"

Swallowing hard, she strove to sound nonchalant. "Joel and Royal are being extra cautious, that's all. We'll be heading to the campground soon, don't worry."

"Does that mean we get to camp in a tent?" Ben appeared enthusiastic at the prospect.

She hid a grimace. The very last thing she

wanted was to spend the night in a tent. The bugs were bad enough during the daytime, and what if the grizzly or other animals came out at night? She didn't even want to think about it. "No, Ben. We're meeting Joel's brother Justin and his dog, Stone. You remember Stone, right? He looks just like Royal only yellow in color. He is a good tracker too."

Ben nodded. She was glad he didn't seem to appreciate the seriousness of the situation. She glanced back at Joel and Royal. The dog hadn't barked, which she took as a good sign.

Joel shot her a reassuring thumbs-up before he disappeared around a large tree to follow Royal. She instantly felt vulnerable being there alone.

Obviously, Joel wasn't far, and Royal hadn't alerted them to danger, but still. She wasn't at home in the wilderness the way Joel was.

The way all the Sullivans were, she reminded herself. They spent most of their time combing through the forest and mountains searching for and rescuing people in need. As if she needed more proof Joel would never fall for someone like her.

And really, she didn't necessarily want to learn about hiking in the woods or finding lost people. Sure, it was an admirable job, but she was convinced she'd only get herself lost in the process.

The seconds ticked by in her head in what

seemed like slow motion. As panic boiled up inside, she heard Joel say, "Okay, boy. Let's go back."

Thank you, Lord Jesus! The prayer came without conscious thought; Joel's influence related to God and faith were rubbing off on her. She forced herself to relax. This level of stress wasn't good for anyone, and she needed Ben to feel safe and secure.

Joel emerged from the trees a few minutes later with Royal at his side. "Okay, we can keep going."

"Great." She injected enthusiasm into her tone. The end of this hike was near, and she was more than ready to get out of the forest to meet up with Justin and Stone. She stepped back, releasing Ben. "Let's go."

Ben didn't need any urging. He ran ahead, swinging his stick like a sword. As far as her nephew was concerned, this was all one big grand adventure.

Not her kind of adventure, although maybe she could incorporate some of this into her next book. She wished she still had her laptop but reminded herself that her work would be there when they reached civilization.

If they reached civilization. Swatting at flies and mosquitos, she hastened to keep up with Joel and Ben.

Ten minutes later, she was relieved to see a couple of bright orange and red tents through the trees. The campground was close now, and seeing signs of other people being close helped to infuse her with strength and determination.

They were going to be fine.

At least for now. The wave of relief quickly dissipated. She had a bad feeling this was a temporary reprieve. Whoever this guy was, he seemed bound and determined to kill her.

But why? Trina had never hurt another person in her life. That some person had decided to target her was unfathomable.

"I'm hungry," Ben announced. "I thought we were having lunch?"

"Soon." Joel glanced at her, a wry smile tugging at the corner of his mouth. "I remember being his age and feeling hungry all the time. Must have a growth spurt coming on."

"I've been reading growth and development books, so I think you're right about that." She flushed a little when he looked amused. "Hey, I needed something to guide me. I was advised not to buy new school clothes until the weather changes."

"I don't need clothes." Ben turned his gaze on her. "But another video game would be awesome."

"We'll see." She made a silent promise that if— no—when the gunman was arrested, she'd buy him two new games.

"Aw, Auntie Trina." Ben kicked at a tree. "Can we at least go back to get my new game?"

"No, Ben." Joel's voice was firm. "But keep in mind you still have your original game at hour house."

"So we can get that one?" Ben brightened.

"Not yet. Soon." She forced a smile. He sure could be insistent. And it seemed as if the impact from the explosion had already worn off.

Joel was right. Kids were resilient. And the only bright side to all of this was that Ben wasn't thinking too much about losing his mother.

Joel pulled his phone from his pocket. "Hey, we're at the campground. What's your ETA?" He listened for a moment, then said, "Great. See you in ten."

"Ten minutes?" She couldn't hide her hopeful tone. When he nodded, she sighed. "That's wonderful."

"Yep." He checked his compass. "Justin asked us to head to the southeast corner of the campground. It's not too far. We headed mostly south for the past mile."

Since she had no idea what direction they'd been going, she didn't argue. Refusing to complain about her aching feet, she quickened her pace to keep up. The sooner they met up with Justin and Stone, the better.

It wasn't the full ten minutes when a yellow dog came running through the woods toward them. Royal's tail wagged with excitement as he bounded after his buddy.

"Stone is leading the way," Joel said with a smile.

Sure enough, a picnic table came into view a moment later. Joel's twin, Justin, was unpacking a large red cooler.

"What are we having for lunch?" Ben asked, bolting straight for the food. "I'm starving."

"Do you like fried chicken?" Justin asked.

Ben's eyes widened as he nodded. "I love fried chicken."

"Who doesn't?" Joel asked.

"I'm in." Any meal she didn't have to cook was fine with her.

Joel grabbed two bottles of water, handing one to her and the other to Ben. "Drink up, we need to stay hydrated."

She gratefully drank half the water, then moved closer. In addition to the fried chicken, it appeared they had mashed potatoes, carrot and celery sticks, along with apples and what looked like chocolate chip cookies for dessert.

"Wow, Anna is a marvel," she said in awe.

"She is." Joel gestured to the picnic table. "Have a seat. Ben, you sit next to your aunt."

As if knowing a meal was forthcoming, both K9s crawled under the picnic table to rest.

"Okay." Ben climbed onto the bench seat. When he reached for a drumstick, she caught his wrist.

"We have to say grace first," she reminded him.

For a second, she feared he'd argue, but when he saw Joel and Justin both bowing their heads, Ben did the same.

She hid a smile.

"Dear Lord Jesus, we ask You to bless this food," Joel said. "We also thank You for keeping us all safe in Your care. Please continue to guide us to safety. Amen."

"Amen," she, Justin, and even Ben echoed.

"Now you can dig in," Justin told Ben. "There are plenty of drumsticks for everyone, so help yourself."

"Yum." Ben took a big bite. "It's good."

Joel and Justin waited for her to fill her plate before diving in. They ate in silence for a few minutes, although she noticed Justin gave Joel a couple of meaningful glances as if they needed to talk.

The meal was delicious. When they'd finished the main meal, Justin handed out cookies. "These are from yesterday, but they're still good."

She was amazed to hear Anna made large meals like this on a regular basis, but then again, the Sullivan siblings were busy saving lives. She imagined they burned zillions of calories on their search and rescue missions.

Maybe she needed to take a more serious approach to hiking.

"Okay, now that we've eaten, what's the plan?" Joel asked.

Ben bent over to look under the table at the pair of K9s. He didn't try to sneak them any food, which was a step in the right direction. Then he glanced up at her. "Aunt Trina, can I play with Royal and Stone?"

She inclined her head toward Joel and Justin. "You need to ask their permission."

"Can I?" Ben repeated.

"Of course," Joel answered without hesitation. "Just stay close. We need to be able to see you at all times."

"Okay!" Ben climbed down from the bench seat. "Come, Royal! Come, Stone!"

The dogs crawled out from beneath the table to chase each other and Ben around the clearing.

"I'd like to know the plan too," Trina said once Ben was out of earshot. "I don't understand why the police haven't been able to find this man yet."

"Griff has been working on it." Justin's expression was somber. "Your ex-boyfriend is still missing in action."

"Robby Rawlings?" Joel asked. When his twin

nodded, he scowled. "I hope the Cody police issued a BOLO for him."

"They have," Justin said. "And from what I hear, the other guy, Peter Thomas, is still MIA as well."

"I don't understand how two men can drop off the face of the earth." She couldn't hide her frustration. "I mean, it shouldn't be that hard to find them."

"It's not difficult to go off the grid in a state as big as Wyoming." Joel grimaced, and added, "But yeah, with technology on our side, I'd think the police should be able to find them pretty quick."

"They're working on it," Justin said. "Griff has been coordinating the law enforcement efforts between Cody and Laramie."

"Knowing Griff, he's just as frustrated by the lack of progress." Joel sighed. "In the meantime, we need another safe place to stay."

"I've already thought of that," Justin agreed. "I've asked a friend of ours, Grady McFarland, if we can use his place. Grady is out of town visiting his sister in Idaho. He said we could use his place no problem."

Joel frowned. "I don't know. What if the gunman finds us there and blows the place up? He seems to like setting fires and using bombs."

"That's the same argument no matter where we end up." Justin shrugged. "I'm open to other ideas."

"Yeah, well, the other problem is that Grady's

place is only a few blocks from where Trina and Ben live." Joel played with his empty water bottle. "That may be too close for comfort."

"Or we could consider that Grady's place is exactly where the gunman would never think to look," Justin countered. "As I said, I'm open to other ideas."

Trina remained silent, deciding it was better to follow Joel and Justin's lead on this. As long as they had a place to stay that wasn't a tent in the middle of the woods, she was all in.

Although it occurred to her that staying in a tent in the woods might be safer. If they weren't mauled by a grizzly. Or attacked by a bobcat or some other ferocious animal.

"Yeah, okay. We'll stay at Grady's." Joel stood and began packing the food containers into the cooler. "I appreciate his help."

"He's a good friend." Justin agreed. "And honestly, if anything bad does happen, I'm sure Maya and Chase will agree to pay for the repairs."

"I can help pay too," she offered. "I'm the reason we're in this mess."

"No need." Joel shook his head as he continued packing. "We'll be fine, especially since we'll be staying off the internet moving forward."

She nodded and wished she didn't feel as if she were a burden to Joel and Justin. Yet she hadn't asked for this. Nobody in their right mind would ask for this.

Turning, she watched as Ben and the dogs played. Then she glanced up at the sky and leaned on prayer for the second time that day.

Please, Lord Jesus, keep Ben safe in Your care.

JOEL STILL WASN'T THRILLED with the idea of being in a house so close to where Trina and Ben lived, but maybe his twin was right about that being the last place the bad guy would look for them.

As he hauled the cooler to Justin's SUV, he frowned. "We need to stop and get a rental car."

"Why?" Justin glanced at the dogs. "Our vehicles are designed for K9s."

"I know that, but it's occurred to me that the K9 crate might be too noticeable." He gestured to the back hatch.

"Come on, Joel." His brother cocked his head. "I can't imagine the gunman is out there searching for SUVs that are designed to transport dogs."

"My SUV was blown to bits," he shot back. "We were either found via the internet somehow or the SUV. I'm not sure which."

Justin sighed. "Okay, look, if you want to get a

rental, that's fine. But just understand you won't have all your K9 gear if needed."

Joel hesitated as that sank in. Maybe his brother was right. He could try to haul everything from Justin's SUV to the rental, but it wouldn't be the same.

"I'm not sure what to do," he confessed in a low voice. Trina had walked over to chat with Ben, so he glanced at his brother. "I've never been in a situation like this. I feel like nothing I do is good enough to keep them safe."

"Hey, don't forget you have God on your side." Justin clapped a hand on his shoulder. "And they're safe now because of you."

Yeah, but for how long? He didn't voice his concern.

"Now that I think about it, we can move stuff around in Grady's garage," Justin said. "I know he doesn't routinely park his truck in there, but I'm sure we can make room for the SUV."

"That might work." The plan cheered him up. "Hopefully, Grady doesn't get upset."

Justin waved that off. "You know he's easygoing most of the time. Not sure why he'd care if we took the time to reorganize his garage."

Cleaning the space would take some time, but he had to believe they had a head start. Whoever had blown up his SUV hadn't followed them into the woods. So maybe, just maybe they could get back to Cody and get situated in Grady's place before this guy realized where they'd gone. He nodded. "Okay, let's go to work."

"Now you're talking." Justin grinned. "We just need to cram everything into the SUV for the trip into town."

"We'll manage." He already felt better having a solid plan. His twin was right; they could make this work. "Royal, come!"

His K9 instantly whirled toward the sound of his voice. Then Royal trotted to his side.

"You too, Stone," Justin called. The yellow lab obediently came to his side.

"Where are we going?" Ben asked as he and Trina followed the dogs to the SUV. "Will there be video games there?"

"Nope, but there will be a television." Joel forced a reassuring smile. Grady wasn't one for gaming, and even if he had been, it wasn't likely Grady would have anything suitable for young kids. "We'll get your game from your house once it's safe."

"Okay." That promise appeased Ben for the moment. Joel was learning that the vague answers Trina often gave Ben were the best way to handle the boy's constant questions.

The longer he spent time with Trina and Ben, the more his admiration for her grew. Not only had she stepped in to take custody of her nephew, but she'd read who knew how many books to prepare herself for instant parenthood.

Trina was so different from the women he'd dated. Women, he silently acknowledged, who had plenty of outward beauty but lacked the sweet goodness deep within.

Not that he was ready to settle down. Still, he couldn't help but realize how Trina had been forced into doing that, regardless of whether she was ready for a family or not.

Giving himself a mental shake, he opened the back passenger door. "Trina, you and Ben sit in the back with Royal. Stone will stay in the crate, and I'll ride up front with Justin."

"Yay! I love Royal!" Ben clamored inside, patting the seat beside him. "Come on, Royal. Get up!"

Joel gave Royal the hand signal to jump in. Royal gracefully leaped onto the back seat, then gave Ben a lick on his cheek.

"Royal, that tickles," Ben said with a giggle.

The boy's laughter eased the tension from his shoulders. Maybe he wasn't doing the best job of protecting them, but as his brother pointed out, they were alive and unharmed. Physically, at least. Emotionally, he knew this was taking a toll on Trina. Ben seemed to be doing okay so far.

Yet he couldn't stand the thought of failing

them. Two innocent people who'd done nothing to warrant this level of anger and fury.

He closed the rear door and slid into the front passenger seat.

Please, Lord Jesus, give me the strength and wisdom I need to do this!

On the heels of that prayer, a familiar Bible verse flashed in his mind. *I can do everything through Christ who strengthens me. (Philippians 4:13)*

He relaxed against the seat, feeling better.

"Everyone set?" Justin put the SUV in gear and pulled out of the picnic space.

"Take the back roads into Cody if possible." Joel glanced at his brother. "And avoid going past Trina's house."

Justin cocked a brow. "That was my plan."

Joel knew his brother was smart enough to figure that out for himself, but for some reason, the thought of returning to Cody concerned him. Not that using a cabin in the middle of the woods had worked.

All he could do now was stay focused. He needed to trust that Griff and the local police would find one or both of their suspects very soon.

They were on the road for barely five minutes when Ben said, "I have'ta go to the bathroom."

Of course he did. That was something Joel

should have anticipated. "We'll stop at the first gas station we find, okay?"

"Okay." He glanced back to see the little boy was wiggling in his seat. One look at Trina's brown eyes had him leaning forward. "Find a bathroom soon, Justin."

"On it." Even as his brother spoke, Justin hit the gas. The SUV surged forward. Two long minutes passed before a gas station sign came into view.

"We're almost there." Joel gave Trina and Ben a reassuring smile. "See? There's the gas station."

"Hurry," Ben urged, still wiggling.

Justin pulled into the parking lot. Before Joel could get out, Ben had his door open and was running toward the gas station. Joel glanced briefly at Trina, then slid out and hurried after him.

The restrooms were located toward the back. Somehow, Ben had found it because the door was already closed and locked.

He stood nearby to wait. It didn't take long for him to hear the sound of a toilet flushing and water running in the sink.

Ben emerged looking sheepish.

"Buddy, you can't wait until it's an emergency," he told him. "What if we couldn't find a gas station?"

Ben lifted his thin shoulders. "I was playing with the dogs."

Joel sighed. He supposed this was another part

of parenting. They should have used the restrooms at the campground before leaving. "Okay, let's go." He guided the boy back outside.

Sweeping his gaze across the parking lot, he didn't see anything alarming. Reassured, he followed Ben to the SUV.

The rest of the trip into Cody via the back roads was uneventful. Justin pulled up to Grady's small home and killed the engine, giving Joel a quick glance. "Why don't you get Trina and Ben inside before we work on the garage. Front door key is hidden within the light fixture."

He nodded and pushed out of the vehicle. Finding the key wasn't difficult, and inside, he was reassured to note Grady's home was clean and comfortable.

"Hey, my friend Mitch lives over there." Ben gestured to the home across the street. "Can I play with him?"

"Not now, maybe later." Trina looked worn out. "Let's find something to watch on television, okay?"

Ben heaved a sigh, but since Royal and Stone had joined them in the house, he was easily distracted. The dogs followed him into the living room where he found the remote.

Trina walked into the kitchen. "I don't know about you, but I could use some coffee."

"Sounds good." He tucked his hands in his front

pockets and leaned against the door jamb. "I didn't realize Ben had a friend living close by."

"Me either." She glanced over her shoulder at him. "I mean, I knew Mitch lived there, but I didn't know your friend had a place across the street."

"Maybe we should find another place to stay." He grimaced. "Ben will keep asking to play with Mitch, but we can't allow that. Not until this guy is behind bars."

"I know. We'll just keep putting him off. At least for the rest of the day." She shrugged as she found the coffee. "This town is small enough that we probably can't stay much longer than that anyway without being noticed."

She had a point. People were out in the summer more so than during the long cold winter months. He pushed away from the doorway. "I need to help clear out the garage."

Trina nodded and continued making coffee. As he turned to open the connecting garage door, Joel hoped and prayed staying there would work out.

He couldn't afford to make any more mistakes.

13

———————

Glancing over to where Ben fiddled with the remote control for the television, Trina tried to stay positive. Being on the run, hiking through the woods, and fearing danger at every turn was wearing her down. Her exhaustion was more mental than physical. And she knew she'd feel this way until this crazed maniac was found and tossed behind bars.

When the coffee pot was full, she poured a cup. Taking a seat at the kitchen table, she reveled in the relative peace and quiet.

Having Ben in her home twenty-four seven had been a huge adjustment. She used to have plenty of downtime. Now, quiet moments like this were rare.

Not that she regretted her decision to take custody of Ben. She loved him, as much as if he were her own son. He was a good kid who deserved a chance to live his life. And if that meant making sacrifices, so be it. Besides, things would no doubt be better once he started back to school.

Two and a half weeks and counting.

"Can I play with Mitch tomorrow?" Ben asked.

She forced a smile. "We'll see."

He flopped back onto the sofa with a loud sigh. "You always say that."

She did, so there was no point in arguing. "Did you find something to watch on TV?"

"Not yet." Her attempt at a distraction worked. He lifted the remote and began searching stations. "But I don't think it's fair that I can't have my video game or play with Mitch."

Since she didn't want to remind him of the danger, there wasn't much she could say. Thankfully, Ben was focused on the television. Why he wasn't tired out from what they'd been through was a mystery. She was learning that kids seemed to have boundless energy.

Taking another minute to enjoy her coffee, she finally set it aside. Rising to her feet, she poked around in the fridge and freezer. They'd had a huge lunch, the most delicious fried chicken she'd ever tasted in her life, but knowing Ben, he'd still be ready for dinner in a few hours.

It felt a little like she was invading Grady McFarland's personal life by looking around in his fridge. Not that food was private, per se. Yet she'd never met Grady. In fact, she didn't remember him from high school either. Although if he was a year older like Joel and Justin, she might not have paid attention.

It was nice of him to share his home. She made a mental note to ask Joel if they could reimburse him for the groceries they'd use. And for anything else that happened.

She shared Joel's and Justin's concerns about the gunman finding them there and causing damage to the house and property. The explosion at the cabin, not to mention the gunfire and arson attempt at her home, remained fresh in her mind.

Finding a couple of frozen pizzas in the freezer, including a cheese and pepperoni, Ben's favorite, she decided they'd have that for dinner. Easy and practical worked for her.

The door from the garage opened, and Joel walked in. He flashed a smile as he headed for the coffee pot. "The SUV is in the garage. We're safe here."

"Great." His smile made her wish for things she'd never have.

"Are you okay?" He eyed her over the rim of his mug. "I know it's been a difficult morning."

"Of course." She returned to her seat at the table. Difficult was an understatement, but other than having sore feet from hiking, she was fine. And more importantly, Ben had shaken off his initial fears to bounce back to his usual self. "Where's Justin?"

"He's looking around the property." Joel sipped his coffee. "Grady has almost a full acre of land here. He's just checking things out."

She cupped her hands around her mug. "I really wish this was over. It's hard to be so close to my home without being able to go inside."

"I feel for you." His gaze was sympathetic. "I'm going to call Griff soon. We really could use an update."

She bit her lip to avoid a sarcastic response. It was depressing to know there was little to no progress on the case in the past twenty-four hours. Sure, this was real life, not one of her mystery stories, but she had expected more.

"Don't despair," Joel said in a low voice. "Griff and the local police will come through for us soon."

She nodded, forcing a smile. "I know. It just seems incredulous that this guy has been able to slip through their fingers for so long."

"It bugs me too." He grimaced and took another sip. "I doubt Peter Thomas or Robby Rawlings can stay off the grid for long. They're bound to be found eventually."

She hoped he was right about that. Finishing her coffee, she rose to set the cup in the sink. Joel moved over but was still close enough that she caught his musky scent. There was something about him that called to her senses.

He was the wrong guy for her by a mile, but that didn't seem to stop her senses from going on high alert when he was near. This forced togetherness wasn't helping either.

She wanted—no, what was the point of wanting something she couldn't have? She needed to get a grip on her imagination.

Too bad she didn't have her laptop. She was desperate for something to do. Since her laptop wasn't an option, she decided to look for a pad of paper. She normally only used notepads for making notes on her story, preferring to do all her actual writing on the computer. But she was willing to give writing by hand a try if that was the only option available. She had to do something or go crazy.

Something other than walk into Joel's arms, seeking his strength and comfort.

Grady had a pad of paper and several pens in a drawer. She carried them into the living room to sit beside Ben. Royal and Stone were curled up beside him, Royal resting his head on Ben's lap. Ben had found a show to watch and appeared satisfied.

For now.

The next hour passed peacefully enough. Writing longhand wasn't working, but she was able to make notes, outlining her next chapter well enough that she thought this was something she should do more often. It would shorten the time it took her to write a chapter, that's for sure. After a while, Justin came inside and helped himself to coffee too. Stone opened one eye, looked toward Justin, then closed it again. Royal didn't budge.

When the twins sat at the table to talk, she set the notepad aside and crossed over to join them. Their discussion likely impacted her and Ben.

"I left a message with Griff," Joel said as she sat beside him. "Hopefully, he'll call back soon."

Justin nodded. "Maybe he's interviewing one of our suspects."

"Trina, would you like coffee?" Joel asked.

"No thanks." She sighed. "I don't like sitting around doing nothing."

"Trust me, this isn't our norm either." Joel reached over to lightly touch her arm. "At least Ben is quiet."

"I know he can't play with Mitch, but he's not going to stop asking." For being eight, her nephew could be stubbornly determined when he wanted to be. "If we don't know anything by tomorrow, it will get even worse."

The twins exchanged a long look. Justin gave a

slight nod. "I know. I can imagine he'll be relentless. We'll just have to deal with it."

Easy for him to say, she thought with a scowl.

Joel's phone rang. He showed the screen with Griff's name and answered. "Hey, Griff, please tell me you have news."

"Put the call on speaker," Justin suggested.

Joel nodded. "Hang on, Griff, Justin and Trina are here and need to hear this too." He put the call on speaker and set it in the middle of the table. "Go ahead, Griff. Tell us what you know."

"Okay, so it's a good news, bad news situation," Griff said. "The Cody police found Robby Rawlings. He went on a bender and happened to be staying with a buddy of his, Tyson Cutler. It wasn't one of the names you gave us, so it took longer for us to track him down."

"What caused him to drink himself into oblivion?" Joel asked. "Was it the breakup?"

"According to Rawlings, yes." There was a pause, then Griff added, "We've spoken to his ex-girlfriend who confirmed the story the bartender gave us."

"I only met Tyson a few times," Trina said. "But to be honest, I didn't much like him. If you ask me, he'd say whatever Robby wanted him to."

"I got that same impression, Trina," Griff agreed. "We spent the past hour verifying Rawlings's alibi. We have video from the liquor store where they bought their booze and tracked down a sandwich delivery driver who dropped off food at Tyson's address. I hate to admit this, but I believe them. Tyson's trailer house was a disaster. It looked to me as if they didn't leave other than to get liquor."

Trina couldn't say she was surprised by the news that Robby wasn't the person responsible. It had been a stretch to imagine he'd go so far as to shoot at her, start a fire, and then put a bomb beneath Joel's SUV.

But Griff was right that this was bad news. They were still no closer to identifying the gunman. And without that, she and Ben weren't free to return home.

"Sounds like we can cross Rawlings off our suspect list," Joel said after a moment. "What's the news on Peter Thomas?"

"I haven't heard back from the Laramie PD," Griff said. "Once I'm finished here, I'm doing to drive down there to talk to them in person."

"How hard can it be to find Peter?" The comment came out before she could stop it, and from the surprised looks on Joel's and Justin's faces, she realized how cranky she sounded. "I'm sorry, Griff, I'm not angry with you. It's just that Ben and I have been in danger nonstop, which has forced us to stay in four different places in the past two days." Her voice broke, and she bit her lip to steady herself.

Then she finally added, "I can't take much more of this."

"Trina, I feel for you and Ben. I wish I could make this process go faster for you." Griff sounded sincere. "I agree it's not right that you've been in danger like this. That's part of the reason I'm heading to Laramie as soon as we're finished here."

She blinked back the urge to cry. Getting angry with Griff wasn't helpful. He was doing his best, as were the local law enforcement. Hard to track down someone who hasn't left the house in three days.

"The Cody PD put out a BOLO on Peter Thomas," Griff said. "Nobody has seen him, and trust me, they've been looking. Makes me think he may have hightailed it back to Laramie."

"After setting the bomb at the cabin?" Joel sounded unconvinced. "I don't think so. These attacks have been coming fast and furious."

"Speaking of the explosion, I need to understand what happened," Griff said.

She would rather he get on the road to Laramie but managed to be patient as Joel filled his brother-in-law in on the sequence of events. "This taught me a hard lesson," Joel said. "We always need to trust our dogs. We should have gotten out of the cabin immediately after Royal's alert." The pained expression in Joel's eyes had her covering his hand with hers. She didn't blame him. She was the one who hadn't wanted to leave.

"Yeah, I hear you. I'm just glad nobody was hurt." Griff's tone sounded grim. "That was too close for comfort. We need to get crime scene techs up there."

"I'll text you the address," Joel said.

"I called Trevor. He's finishing up his search and will arrange to have the damaged SUV towed to a wreckage yard," Justin added. "That will take some time, so your crime scene techs can do their thing first. But we need to figure out the vehicle situation. We have one extra SUV at the ranch, but I've sent a message to Chase that we need to purchase a replacement soon. They take time to get because they're specially made for our K9s."

"Understood," Griff said. "I'll get those techs out there ASAP. Anything else?"

Joel lifted a brow. She shook her head at his unspoken question. "Nothing from me. But will you please let us know when you find Peter?"

"Count on it," Griff promised. "Hang in there, okay?"

Did she have a choice? When Joel ended the call, she abruptly stood and moved away from the brothers. Seeking privacy in the bathroom, she sank onto the commode and buried her face in her hands.

Feeling overwhelmed with anger, fear, and despair, she opened her heart to prayer. It was the only way to obtain the solace she so desperately needed.

And still, it wasn't enough, making her wonder if her prayers fell on deaf ears.

JOEL HATED SEEING Trina so down. He stood and paced the kitchen, waiting for her to return.

"Give her some space, bro," Justin advised. "She's been through a lot."

"I know." It pained Joel to admit he hadn't done enough to keep her and Ben safe.

"My show is over," Ben announced. "Now can I go play with Mitch?"

"No, Ben." Joel kept his tone firm. "We'll talk about that tomorrow, okay?"

Ben rolled his eyes. "I wanna play now."

"I don't think Mitch is home," Justin said. "I was outside earlier, and he and his parents got into their Jeep and drove off."

Ben eyed him suspiciously, then sighed again. "Then I want my video game."

"Maybe tomorrow," Joel said. "If things are quiet tonight, and if you behave yourself, I'll head over to your house to get your game."

"Really?" That perked Ben up. "Promise?"

"I promise." One Joel hoped he wouldn't regret. "You have to hold up your end of the deal."

Ben shrugged as if that was not a problem.

A few minutes passed before Trina emerged from the bathroom. Her eyes looked red, as if she might have been crying, and she avoided his gaze.

He wanted to reassure her but couldn't think of anything to say that didn't sound trite and useless.

"I was thinking of making the frozen pizzas for dinner." She gestured to the fridge. "Grady has two of them. That should be enough for the four of us."

"Sounds good." Joel glanced at his brother. "You have dog food in the SUV, right?"

"Yep." Justin glanced at his watch. "I'll grab the bucket of kibble now, along with their bowls."

As if on cue, both dogs lifted their heads to stare at them. Joel shook his head wryly. "You shouldn't have said the K word."

"No joke." Justin grinned as he moved toward the door. "They crack me up. I'll take the dogs outside in a little while. I suggest we stay out back to avoid curious gazes from the neighbors."

"Understood." Joel agreed. The less attention they drew, the better. He wondered if Justin had really noticed Mitch leaving across the street or if his brother had made that up to keep Ben from harping on it.

Probably the latter, he thought with a shrug. A

white lie that wouldn't hurt Ben and keep the peace for Trina's sake.

Joel offered to cook the pizzas, but Trina jumped to the task. He understood the waiting around was getting to her too.

"Can I go outside with the dogs?" Ben asked when Justin opened the back door to let them out.

"Not now," Joel said. "We're staying inside for the rest of the night."

"Why?" Ben looked upset. "I always get to play outside when it's nice out."

So much for his promise to behave. "Listen, Ben, I know it's hard, but you need to stay inside for today. We hiked this morning, remember?"

"That was hours ago," Ben whined.

"Enough, Ben." Trina sounded a bit on edge. "None of us wants to be cooped up inside, but we don't have a choice."

"We can play card games after dinner," Joel suggested. "Do you know how to play gin rummy?" When Ben shook his head, Joel smiled. "I'll teach you. It will be fun."

When their pizzas were ready, Joel said grace. He noticed Ben watching Justin as this was the second time his twin had joined them in prayer. "Lord Jesus, we ask You to bless this food. We thank You again for keeping us safe in Your care. We continue to ask for strength and guidance during these difficult times. Amen."

"Amen," Justin and Trina echoed.

"Amen," Ben added a second later. "Now we can dig in?"

"Absolutely." Justin put a slice of pepperoni pizza on Ben's plate. "Here you go, big guy."

"Yum!" Ben took an eager bite. Trina flashed his brother a grateful smile. Joel knew she'd been dealing with Ben alone for a few months now and probably appreciated a helping hand.

And the brief flash of jealousy was completely unfounded. He did his best to ignore it. He and Justin had never fought over a woman in their lives. They wouldn't start now.

After dinner, he helped Trina with the dishes. The dogs ran around the kitchen, generally getting in the way. He shooed them into the living room where they eventually settled down to sleep. When they were finished with the kitchen duty, he gestured to the living room. "Why don't you take a break? Justin and I will play cards with Ben."

"Are you sure?" She looked up at him with hope reflected in her brown eyes. "I feel like I should play too."

"Hey, you deserve some downtime." He nodded to where Justin was already explaining the rules of the game. "I doubt Ben will mind if you sit out. We've got this."

"You're sweet, Joel. Thank you." Her smile melted his heart. It was all he could do not to pull her into his arms.

Then she went up on her tiptoes to brush a kiss across his cheek. A brotherly, chaste kiss. Unlike the one they'd shared, what yesterday? It seemed like eons ago.

He watched as she headed back into the living room, picking up her paper and pencil. Forcing himself to stay focused on the mission, he turned to join his twin at the table. "Are we ready?"

"As ever." Justin grinned. The challenge was on.

They played with Ben for a solid hour, taking turns winning, not on purpose, as that wasn't how Sullivans rolled. Unlike the way they banded together to support each other in SAR missions, when it came to family game night, it was every man for himself.

"I like this game," Ben said when he won the last hand.

Trina came over to the table, a genuine relaxed smile on her face. "Okay, Ben, let's get ready for bed."

"Will you tell me a story?" Ben asked as he hopped off the chair.

"Sure." Trina rested a hand on his shoulder. "But let's wash up first."

When they disappeared down the hall, Joel looked at his brother. "I'm going to sleep on the sofa, so you can take one of the bedrooms."

"Nope, I'm taking the sofa. You need to rest." His brother raked a critical eye over him. "Gotta say, you look rough around the edges."

Joel scowled. "I'm fine."

"I'm better than fine. I'm well rested for the most part." Justin slapped him on the back. "You told Trina to take a break, now it's your turn. I'll be out here with Stone. He'll let me know if anything goes wrong."

Joel hesitated, then nodded. They had two watchdogs in the house, which gave him an added measure of comfort. "Okay. Thanks."

"Don't mention it." Justin arched a brow. "I can tell you really like her."

Joel narrowed his eyes. "I do, but we're just friends. I need to stay focused on protecting her."

"Hey, I get that. But once this is done? I think you should take her out for a proper date." Justin punched him lightly in the arm. "She's cute."

She was cute and so was Ben, but he wasn't going there. "Thanks again. Come, Royal." He turned toward the back door. "I'll take a walk around the property outside now too. Best if we know the lay of the land in case this guy somehow finds us."

"There aren't a lot of places for the gunman to hide," Justin observed. "That may work in our favor."

"I hope so." They could use a slight advantage. He and Justin took the dogs outside one last time, walked the perimeter of the lot, then headed back inside.

They were safe, and that would have to be enough for now.

Despite his lack of sleep the past few nights, Joel tossed and turned. Royal snored, and he stared at the ceiling, listening to his dog. He finally drifted off to sleep, only to be awakened by someone shaking his arm.

"Joel, wake up." He opened one eye to see Trina hovering over him, her expression panicked. Royal jumped up and came over to nudge him.

"What's wrong?" He stared up at her. "Ben? Is he sick?"

"He's gone." Her voice hitched. "I think he may have tried to run away again."

"He wouldn't." Joel shot up off the bed. He opened the blinds, surprised to see it was morning, probably close to six thirty. He'd slept in longer than he normally did. "Justin and Stone would have stopped him from leaving."

"He went out the window." Trina's eyes filled with tears. "What if the gunman gets him?"

"Okay, let's not go there yet. I'm sure Ben hasn't gone far." Where would the boy go? Most likely to Mitch's house. Ben had been vocal about wanting to play with his friend. "I'll take Royal, and we'll search for him. I'm sure he's across the street."

"I hope so." Trina gripped his arm tightly. "I can't bear the thought of that madman getting his hands on Ben."

"He won't." Although the image of some guy hauling Ben away at gunpoint was difficult to ignore. "Come, Royal."

He went straight to Ben's room. The open window seemed to indicate that was the route Ben had taken, but he took a moment to address his dog. He patted the bed sheets. "This is Ben. You know Ben, right? Search! Search Ben!"

Royal didn't hesitate to sniff the bed, then around the carpeted floor. His K9 went straight to the window, sniffed, then surprised Joel by vaulting through.

He followed his K9 as the dog searched along the dew-laden grass outside. The dog trotted across the lawn, then headed to the front of the house. When Joel expected Royal to go across the street, the dog surprised him by turning to head down the block, away from Mitch's house.

Trina followed their progress, staying back so as not to interfere. It took a few minutes for him to figure out where Ben had headed.

"He wanted his video game." He turned to Trina. "I'm sure we'll find him at your place."

"Good." She hurried to catch up.

Royal continued following the scent, the moisture along the grass helping to magnify Ben's scent. Three blocks later, they approached Trina's house. The charred front door was closed, and to Joel's eye, the place looked undisturbed.

Royal went straight to the front door, then sat and barked. "Good boy." He hadn't taken the time to grab Royal's stuffed beaver, so he settled for verbal and petting praise. "You're a good boy, Royal." He opened the front door, which wasn't locked, and headed inside. "Ben? Are you here?"

No answer. He quickly moved from room to room, half expecting to find Ben sleeping in his own bed.

But the place was empty. The scent trail had led them there, yet there was no sign of Ben.

14

Entering the house behind Joel and Royal, Trina went straight to Ben's backpack still propped against the wall in the kitchen. Rummaging inside, she found and removed Ben's favorite video game. She wished more than ever she'd have come here to grab the handheld device yesterday.

She turned as Joel and Royal emerged from the bedrooms. The grim expression on Joel's face squeezed her chest. "He's not here?"

"No." He gestured to the game. "If he had come this far, he'd have surely grabbed the game before leaving, right?"

"Yes." She'd thought it was possible Ben had decided to climb into his own bed, but clearly that wasn't the case. Gripping the game tightly, she stared at Joel. "I don't understand. Royal tracked him here, right?"

"Yes. And I trust my dog." He nodded at Royal. "He knows Ben's scent. I need you to call the Cody police, let them know Ben is missing. I'll keep working with Royal. I'm sure he'll pick up Ben's scent." He glanced around the house. "Maybe Ben came here, but then something scared him off?"

Like the gunman? Swallowing hard, she made the call. The dispatcher promised to send the two officers who worked the night shift. The hour was early enough that the day-shift team hadn't reported in to work yet.

Joel brushed past her to head outside. "Come, Royal."

The black lab followed Joel out of the house. She watched as Joel instructed Royal to search for Ben.

Where could Ben have gone? It didn't make any sense that he'd sneaked out of the house, coming all this way without getting his game or anything else from his backpack. She hurried outside. "Maybe he changed his mind and went back to Mitch's house."

Joel nodded. "Maybe. Royal will let us know."

She tried to quell the surge of panic. This was the second time Ben had gone missing, and Royal had found him the first time. Surely the smart K9 would find him again.

Please, Lord Jesus? Her heart squeezed painfully. *Please keep Ben safe in Your care!*

Royal swept his nose over the driveway, trotting toward the road. As Joel stayed close to his dog, a terrible thought hit.

What if someone took Ben away in a car?

"Joel?" She hurried down the driveway where Royal sat and let out a sharp bark. His alert! *No, please, no!* "What if the gunman has him?"

"Good boy, Royal! Good boy!" Joel lavished praise on his K9, glancing up at her with a somber gaze. "I don't want to think the worst, but we can't discount that possibility either."

A red haze of fury clouded her vision. The gunman had her son!

"We have to find him!" Her anger morphed into full-blown panic. "Joel, please! Royal has to keep searching for him!"

Joel nodded. "Search! Search Ben!"

Royal jumped up and went back to work, sniffing the ground and the air to pick up Ben's scent. He headed along the street, sniffing at one spot in particular.

Her pulse kicked up. Maybe Ben hadn't been taken away by car. Maybe he'd gone down the driveway, saw something, and went over to explore.

She hoped Ben had just gone back on the trail rather than being taken away by someone who had tried multiple times to kill her.

Unless kidnapping Ben had been the goal all along.

No, please, no. Please, Lord, don't take Ben away from me.

The sharp wail of sirens filled the air. A Cody police cruiser came around the corner and rolled to a stop at the end of her driveway.

Joel glanced over as the officer slid out of the vehicle. Then he turned his attention back to Royal.

"Are you Ms. Warren?" The officer's name tag read Simmons.

"Yes." She fought to maintain control. "My son, Ben, is missing. Joel Sullivan and his K9, Royal, tracked Ben here to my house. We're staying a few blocks away." She didn't want to get bogged down with the details, but she needed the patrol officer to know the basics about what she'd been going through. "You may have heard we've been targeted by gunfire, and someone tried to start my house on fire. I'm worried the person who did those things now has Ben. He—" Her voice hitched. "He's only eight years old."

Simmons nodded. "I'm aware of your case. I asked the dispatch to put a call into Sergeant Howell. When's the last time you saw Ben?"

"Last night." She didn't want to stand there talking, but she forced herself to go along with the questions. "I made up a bedtime story, and he fell asleep, maybe around eight thirty or so."

"And when did you realize he was missing?" Simmons asked.

"Six twenty. I woke up and went in to check on him. The window was open, and he was gone."

Simmons arched a brow. "Does Ben often climb out the window?"

"No. But he did try to run away two mornings ago." It seemed like eons since this nightmare started. Her tone rose defensively. "He's still getting used to living with me here in Cody. He lost his mother, my sister, three months ago. I'm his guardian." A flash of impatience hit hard. "None of that matters now. I need you and the other officers to be out there looking for him!"

Joel crossed over to put his arm around her waist. "Have faith, Trina. Justin and Stone will be here soon. I told them to use Ben's pillowcase as a scent source and to meet us here. We'll spread out and search the neighborhood."

"Thank you." She was grateful to have two experienced K9s searching for her nephew. But she couldn't help but think that if the gunman had taken Ben via car, they could be anywhere.

Even another state.

Panic threatened to overwhelm her again. She'd never experienced a fear as raw as this.

Joel turned to Simmons. "Did the other officers who did the canvass after the arson attempt learn anything from Trina's neighbors?"

"I'm not sure. I didn't hear anything about it during roll call last night." Simmons looked cha-grined as if he wished he knew more. "Sergeant Howell will be here soon. You can ask him."

Joel turned his gaze to her. "I'm calling Griff. He needs to know about this."

She nodded. If she could shout the news from the top of the mountain, she would. Every single person in Cody should be searching for her son. That's how she thought about him, she dimly real-ized. He was her son. And she couldn't bear the thought of losing him.

Joel walked away to make the call. She swung her gaze around the familiar area. If one of her neighbors had found Ben, they'd have taken him inside. Maybe he was right now having breakfast at one of the houses nearby?

On the heels of that thought, though, she real-ized that was impossible. Her neighbors were close enough to see them standing out there with the po-lice. They'd know she was searching for Ben.

And the scent trail had stopped at the end of the driveway.

The seconds dragged by as Joel spoke to Griff. Justin and Stone showed up just as Joel finished.

"I'm sorry, Trina." Justin looked upset. "I didn't hear Ben leave. And neither did Stone."

"It's not your fault." The blame for this rested squarely on the gunman's shoulders. "But we need to find him."

"We will." Justin sounded as determined as Joel. She tried to believe they could do this. That God would protect Ben long enough for them to find him.

"Griff is on his way." Joel turned to his brother. "We'll split up the neighborhood. Maybe someone gave Ben a ride to their house."

"I'll go east; you head west." Justin shrugged out of his backpack. "By the way, I brought Royal's stuffed beaver."

"Thanks." Joel gratefully took the toy. "Royal tracked him to the house and down the driveway. Maybe we walk along the road for a while. Could be that Ben changed his mind and decided to back-track to Mitch's home after all."

"I'll call Mitch's mother." She patted her pockets, belatedly realizing she didn't have her phone. Joel had told her it was important to stay off-grid, so she'd turned it off and left it behind. "Joel, I need your phone."

He passed the device, then set about revving up

his dog. Justin had brought the collapsible water bowl, too, and they took turns giving their dogs the opportunity to drink. She called Mary, Mitch's mother, who verified Ben was not there with Mitch.

Her heart squeezed with fear as she handed Joel's phone back.

Justin opened the bag containing the pillowcase Ben had used. "Ben. This is Ben. Search!"

The yellow lab buried his nose in the bag, then began to search. Meanwhile, Joel already had Royal working on the west side of her home.

Feeling entirely helpless and useless, Trina watched the dogs do their thing. But what if that didn't work? What if the gunman had already taken Ben far away from here?

Would Ben have willingly gotten into a car with a stranger? If so, what else had she failed to teach him?

She jammed her fingers through her hair, desperately trying to think. Maybe she should head over to her neighbors to talk to them. There's no reason they wouldn't cooperate with the police, but she couldn't just stand there doing nothing.

Turning, she was about to cross the lawn when Joel's sharp tone broke into her intense thoughts.

"Stop, Royal! Heel!" She frowned, wondering what was going on. His black lab spun around and came instantly to his side, sitting and staring up at him expectantly.

"What is it? What's wrong?" Trina hurried forward. "Why did you call him back?"

"Do you smell that?" Joel waved a hand in the air. "Bleach. Someone used bleach on the road."

Her temper snapped. "So what? I don't care about bleach."

He reached for her hand. "The scent of bleach will ruin a dog's ability to smell anything for at least thirty to forty minutes."

"We have bleach over here too," Justin called out.

Joel's eyes narrowed. "Spilling bleach on the road on both sides of your house wasn't done by accident."

She stared at him in horror. "You mean someone purposefully used bleach here to prevent Royal from tracking Ben?"

"That's my theory." He rested his hand on Royal's head. "Justin, what are your thoughts?"

"Same." Justin came back to her driveway with Stone at his side. "This was done intentionally to cover their tracks."

Her knees threatened to buckle. If they were right, there was no doubt in her mind that the gunman had Ben.

All she could do now was pray the madman who

had him kept her son alive long enough for the K9s to find him.

"EASY." Joel slipped his arm around Trina's waist. She'd gone deathly pale, the freckles across her nose standing out starkly against her skin. She swayed as if a strong wind would blow her over. He tightened his grip when she gratefully leaned against him. "We're going to find him."

"How?" Her voice was an agonized whisper. "How will you find him?"

It was a good question, and he glanced over to Justin for ideas. He'd caught the bleach smell early enough to protect Royal's ability to track, but he wasn't sure where to go from there.

"What did Griff say?" Justin asked.

"The Laramie PD hasn't found Peter Thomas." He frowned. "Although I have to be honest, I would expect Ben to put up a fight if he saw Peter."

"Not if Peter had a gun," Trina said grimly. "And Peter could have threatened to hurt me or one of your dogs."

He nodded. "Okay, so Peter is still a possibility. But then, why would he use bleach on the road?"

"I'm starting to wonder if this isn't the work of someone who lives in the area," Justin said. "And it's strange this gunman just happened to show up here when Ben sneaked out to get his game."

"Are you saying there's a tracking device on Ben?" Trina asked, her eyes wide.

"No, I don't see how anyone could have done that," Joel hastened to reassure her. "But it makes me think the gunman may have been keeping an eye on your home thinking we'd eventually return."

"And used the bleach trick to throw us off," Justin added.

Yeah, Joel had to admit he didn't like this latest twist. That the gunman knew to use bleach in the first place to mess with their K9s indicated this was part of a well thought out plan. And for all they knew, there were other areas nearby where bleach had been used to ruin the ability to track Ben's scent. They may not find it before one of the K9s took a large sniff.

"We have to do something." Trina's voice was thin. "What's our next step?"

He glanced at his brother. But before he could say anything, his twin read his thoughts.

"I agree, we should start by canvassing the neighbors." Justin gestured to the road. "I find it interesting that the bleach pretty much covers the front of the two houses on either side of this one. Someone must have seen something."

"Fine with me, but let's take a police officer with

us." Joel nodded to where the second squad had joined the first. "We need to consider the possibility we're walking into a trap."

"Roger that," Justin muttered.

"My neighbors wouldn't do this." Trina sniffled and swiped fresh tears from her eyes. "They're nice people."

Maybe, maybe not. At this point, Joel considered just about everyone in the entire city of Cody to be a potential suspect.

"Who lives here?" Joel gestured to the house behind him.

"Martha and Frank Vine." A flash of annoyance darkened her eyes. "They're in their fifties, no reason for either one of them to take Ben." She waved at the other house. "And Lisa lives alone."

A chill snaked down his spine. "Lisa who?"

Trina sniffed again. "I don't know her last name. She's new, just moved in a couple of weeks ago."

His gut clenched. "What does she look like? Blond? Pretty?"

"Yes, she's blond and very pretty." Trina pulled away from him to look at him. "Do you know her?"

"I might." And if his gut instinct was right, this was about him, not Trina and Ben.

Justin's eyes widened in alarm. "You're not thinking Lisa Schilling is behind this?"

He nodded, his heart thumping against his ribs.

"Simmons! Come with me." He didn't wait for the cop, but quickly crossed the lawn, giving the bleached area of the road a wide berth. Royal stayed at his side.

He pulled his weapon. To his surprise, Simmons didn't comment on his gun. Either because he was a Sullivan or because just about everyone in Wyoming carried a sidearm.

There was no movement through the windows that he could see. Was Lisa inside with Ben right now? They knew she was armed; she'd already fired at them several times. He went up to the door and tried the knob. It was locked. That alone was suspicious. He pounded on the door. "Lisa? It's Joel Sullivan. Open up!"

There was no answer.

He banged his fist on the door again. "Lisa, open up! It's over! I'm here. You send Ben out safely, and we'll talk."

Still no response. He was fast losing patience and turned to Simmons. "Back me up, I'm going to kick the door in."

"You can't do that. We don't have probable cause!" Simmons protested.

"Yes, we do. Lisa Schilling has been upset with me since I told her I'm not interested in dating her. She has been calling or texting nonstop for the past three weeks since Justin and I rescued her from a hiking trail in the Bighorn Mountains. The last time she called me was two days ago, the morning I was driving here to find Ben when he ran away. I had no idea she lived next door to Trina and Ben. I'm telling you, she's been irrationally persistent." So much so that he'd almost blocked her number. Except he hadn't needed too.

Because he hadn't heard a peep from Lisa since that call he'd sent to voice mail.

When Simmons didn't say anything, Joel made the decision on his own. He lifted his foot and kicked at the doorjamb. Once, twice . . . the third time, the door swung open.

Simmons muttered a curse under his breath as Joel stepped across the threshold, holding his weapon up in a two-handed grip. He swept his gaze and the nose of the gun from side to side, searching for Lisa and/or Ben.

Royal followed him into the house, then sat and barked.

He wanted to believe Royal was alerting to Ben having been there within the past hour. "Good boy," he praised. But he didn't reward the K9 with the beaver. "Search! Search for Ben!"

Royal went to work, sniffing around the kitchen table. Joel pushed forward. It only took a moment to ascertain the main living space was empty.

A sense of urgency hit hard as he moved farther

into the room. Royal darted ahead of him, but rather than going into either of the bedrooms, his K9 stopped to sniff at the base of the back door.

Then he sat and barked.

"Clear the house," he told Simmons over his shoulder. "Royal is telling me they went out the back."

"Are you sure?" Simmons demanded.

"Yes." He trusted Royal. Now that he knew Lisa was involved, he could easily imagine her surprise when she looked outside and saw Ben. He figured Ben wouldn't put up a fuss if she asked him to come to her place. And maybe they'd even walked down the driveway and along the road. Then Lisa had used the bleach to hide the scent trail.

Had she bailed from the house when the police arrived? He shoved open the back door and scanned the backyard. There was no sign of Lisa or Ben.

"Search for Ben," he called to Royal. The dog wagged his tail and went to work, sniffing along the grass, picking up speed as they crossed the dew-laden lawn.

Joel followed his dog, aware that Justin and Stone had joined him. When Simmons didn't immediately follow, as he was still clearing the house, he gave his twin a nod of thanks and let Royal take the lead.

How much of a head start did Lisa have? And

was her anger really just because he hadn't returned her calls?

No, more than that. It was because she was jealous. Stupidly, ridiculously jealous. He clearly remembered how he and Trina had embraced on the hiking trail, moments before the first episode of gunfire had rung out. And then Trina had hugged and kissed him when he'd been about to leave her house. That had brought on the second episode of gunfire.

From there, he had to assume Lisa had simply lost her mind. Deciding to wreak havoc on Trina because she viewed the woman as a rival.

Royal abruptly switched directions, heading toward the hiking trail. It was early enough that he hoped there wouldn't be a lot of people out and about. Much like the day he'd come to search for Ben. Lisa was armed, and based on her escalating tactics, including how she'd set a bomb beneath the SUV, he didn't doubt she'd resort to violence again.

He wasn't sure where Lisa had learned about setting bombs. It was hard to imagine her doing such a thing. Unless she'd had help. It wouldn't surprise him to learn she'd convinced some guy to do the dirty work for her.

Yet she must have been close by, as Royal had alerted on her scent near the creek.

He shoved thoughts of his mistakes away. The

only thing that mattered now was finding Lisa and Ben. Keeping his eye on Royal, he jogged to keep up. He held his weapon in a two-handed grip, but he kept the muzzle pointed at the ground as he moved across the landscape.

Royal stopped near the narrow opening between the trees, sat, and barked. He frowned, assailed by a wave of doubt. Ben had come this way two days ago, was Royal alerting on a recent scent? Or an old one?

Trust your dog. The trainer's voice echoed in the back of his mind.

"Good boy, Royal!" He caught up to his K9. "Good boy, search! Search Ben!"

Despite not getting his toy, Royal jumped up, his tail wagging, and darted through the trees. He followed, glad to know Justin and Stone were covering his flank. Hopefully, Simmons was bringing reinforcements too.

When they reached the hiking trail, Royal turned south. It was the downhill path, which made sense. There was more foliage, twists, and turns in that direction, whereas the northern route led to a parking lot and the possibility of other people being nearby.

Royal stopped again to sniff in a particular area but then continued on his path. As the dog picked up his pace, he heard a rustling in the trees. A sense of alarm hit hard.

"Royal, here!" His sharp tone stopped his K9 in his tracks.

"I had a feeling you'd find me." The familiar sound of Lisa's voice sent a chill down his spine. She emerged from the brush holding Ben in front of her with a gun to his temple. The boy had clearly been crying, but Joel couldn't afford to let that distract him.

"You've seen Royal in action before, remember? When he rescued you." He didn't dare point his gun at her, not when she had her weapon pressed against Ben's head. "It's over, Lisa. Let him go."

Her eyes flashed. "It's over when I say it's over."

It went against the grain, but he nodded. "You're right, Lisa. You're in control here. How about you let Ben go so we can talk?"

"Talk?" She let out a bitter laugh. "Oh, now you want to talk to me? After ignoring my calls for the past ten days?"

"I'm sorry about that. It was rude of me not to take your calls." He tried to hold her gaze, to connect with her in some way. "I treated you badly, Lisa. But that's no reason to make a child suffer."

"She's the reason you ignored me, isn't she?" Lisa's eyes flashed with anger. "She's not even pretty."

Lisa was wrong about that, he was far more attracted to Trina than to this woman standing before him. And that was true even before he knew how crazy Lisa was.

"You don't need Ben," he said. "Take me. You can hold me at gunpoint, okay? I'll trade places with Ben."

Her eyes narrowed. Hopefully, she was considering his proposal. "Throw down your gun."

He did so without hesitation. "Okay, I'm unarmed. You can hold your weapon on me. Just let Ben go."

"Tell your dog to stay back." Lisa scowled at the black lab who had barked at her and was now sitting and staring at her intently. Joel wished Royal was an attack dog, like Shane's Bryce. But he didn't want Royal to be hurt either. "Or I'll shoot him too."

"Even after he saved your life?" When she didn't so much as flinch, he decided she was beyond reason. "Royal, heel." The dog didn't move for a long second, then he finally turned to trot to his side. "Stay, boy. Stay."

Royal sat, looking up at him, then over to Ben.

"Take me, Lisa." Joel took a step forward. And then another. "Take me. I'm the one you're mad at. Take me and let Ben go."

After what seemed like an eternity, she abruptly turned the nose of her gun toward him. "Fine. Run away, Ben."

Ben darted away from Lisa, heading straight for Royal.

Joel took another hasty step forward, putting his body between Lisa and Ben. If she fired now, she'd kill him.

And that would be okay because he knew Justin would make sure to guide Ben back to Trina.

Saving Ben was all that mattered.

15

Trina had followed Justin, Stone, and Officer Simmons, who were in turn trailing Joel and Royal. Learning that her new neighbor Lisa was responsible for these deadly attacks was staggering. She couldn't imagine why this woman would hate her so much to do such terrible things.

Hearing Joel call her pretty had hurt. Yet the description was accurate. She understood Lisa was exactly the type of woman Joel would be attracted to.

Although she'd overheard him saying something to Officer Simmons about how he hadn't wanted to date Lisa. It sounded like the woman had been calling him a lot over the past few weeks. It's probably a good thing Joel stayed away as it was obvious the woman was mentally disturbed.

"Take me, Lisa. I'm the one you're mad at. Let Ben go." Joel's deep voice had caught her attention. She sucked in a quick breath, craning her neck to see what was going on. She couldn't see Lisa, Ben, or Joel. Justin and Simmons were a few yards ahead of her.

Justin turned to place a finger over his lips, indicating she should stay quiet. She nodded in understanding. The last thing she wanted to do was to distract Joel from facing off with this mad woman.

"Come closer, Joel." Lisa's voice was tight. "Don't try anything funny. One wrong move and I'll shoot."

"I understand." How Joel managed to sound so calm in the face of a crisis, she had no idea. Her heart ached. As much as she wanted Ben back, she didn't want to risk losing Joel forever either. What if that nutty woman shot him? Lisa had done so many horrible things, Trina would not put anything past her.

She tensed when Justin eased his weapon from his holster. Was he far enough back that Lisa couldn't see him? Simmons had his weapon out, too, and she tried to find their readiness to take Lisa down reassuring.

But it was worrisome to think Joel could be caught in the cross fire.

Suddenly Ben came running toward her. Tears

flowed from his eyes, and he launched himself into her waiting arms. "Mommy," he choked.

Mommy! He'd called her Mommy. She swept him up and turned to carry him back up the trail, desperate to put distance between them and Justin, Simmons, and Joel.

She couldn't afford to be a distraction.

"Shh, Ben, it's okay. I'm here. You're safe now," she whispered in his ear, still worried about Lisa overhearing them. "It's all over."

"S-she was gonna shoot me." The words came out between sobs.

"I know, but she can't hurt you now." She pressed a kiss to his temple, thankful beyond words that Ben wasn't hurt. At least physically. Emotionally was another story. As if the poor boy didn't have enough trauma in his life after losing his mother. Now he had to relive this nightmare too. "We're going to find the other police officers, okay?"

Ben nodded but then lifted his head. "What about Royal?" He turned to look at the path behind them. "I want to see Royal."

Her stomach twisted with fear and worry. "Royal is with Joel. They're going to get that gun away from Lisa, okay?"

"Are you sure?" Desperation flashed in her son's eyes. "What if she hurts them?"

She drew in a shaky breath and dropped to her

knees. Ben had voiced her greatest fear, and there was very little she could do or say to reassure him. Except for the one thing she knew Joel would appreciate. "We're going to pray right now to Jesus to keep them safe, okay?"

Ben swiped at his face and nodded.

"Dear Lord Jesus, we beg You to keep Joel, Royal, Justin, and Stone safe in Your loving arms. Amen."

"Amen," Ben echoed. "Can Jesus really do that?"

"Yes. Through Him all things are possible." The words that might be from a Bible passage flashed in her mind. She rose and pulled Ben close. "Come with me. We're going to talk to the policemen."

They'd barely taken two steps up the path when the sound of a gunshot rang out. Trina gasped and whirled, fearing the worst. She wanted to go back to see what was happening, but she had to put Ben first.

"Did she kill Royal?" Ben asked.

She helplessly shook her head and forced herself to sound confident. "I'm sure she didn't."

Two police officers ran toward them. The older of the two looked relieved to see her and Ben standing there.

"We're fine," she said quickly. "Go that way, Lisa had Joel at gunpoint."

The officers nodded and continued down the

path. She stood for a moment, straining to listen. She desperately wanted to believe Joel was okay.

The not knowing was killing her.

"Get down!" The shout almost had her dropping to her knees again, until she realized the command was related to someone else. Lisa? She squeezed her eyes closed, silently praying Joel was okay.

For long seconds she didn't move. Her instincts were to get Ben far away, but she couldn't make herself leave.

Not without knowing . . .

"Trina?" Justin and Stone ran toward her. Ben dropped to embrace Stone. "Joel is fine; it's only a flesh wound. The good news is that Lisa is in custody."

"Thank You, Lord Jesus," she whispered. Then she managed a smile. "I appreciate you coming back to tell us."

"I knew you'd be worried after hearing the gunfire." Justin's grin faded. "That was a close call, though. If Joel hadn't anticipated her move, the outcome could have been much worse."

She wished she could see Joel, hug him, and hold him close one last time. He'd put his life on the line for her and most importantly for Ben. He was by far the most honorable man she'd ever met. And despite knowing he thought Lisa was pretty, she still secretly wished for something she couldn't have.

Yet she was grateful for her blessings. That the danger was over for good. That was all she could really ask for. Joel and Royal, along with Justin and Stone, would head back to the Sullivan K9 Search and Rescue Ranch for a well-deserved rest.

She wouldn't stalk him the way Lisa apparently had.

"Let me go! I didn't hurt anyone, let me go!" The shrill voice coming from behind her made her wince. Ben rose from where he'd been hugging Stone to come back to her side.

"That's her," he whispered. "She's scary."

"Yes." She wrapped her arm around him. "But don't worry. The police have her in handcuffs. She won't hurt you ever again."

"Good." Ben lifted his red eyes to her. "Can we go home now?"

"Of course." She caught Justin's gaze. "Thank you, for everything."

Justin nodded, then glanced over his shoulder. "Here's Joel and Royal now."

Ben broke free of her embrace and ran toward the pair. Joel smiled at her, ignoring the blood trickling down his arm. She managed a weak smile back as Royal galloped toward Ben, greeting him with a wildly wagging tail and attempts to lick him in the face.

Despite her internal lecture to let him go, she

found herself walking toward him, increasing her pace until she was within arm's reach. She wrapped her arms around him, hugging him tightly. "Thank you for saving Ben," she whispered. "I'm so glad you weren't badly hurt."

"Anytime." His husky voice sent shivers down her spine. In that moment, she could almost understand Lisa Schilling's obsession.

Almost.

She held him tight for a long moment, then forced herself to release him. "I owe you more than I can ever repay."

"Funny, I was just thinking this is all my fault." Joel frowned as the officers led Lisa away in handcuffs. "She lashed out at you because of me."

"Because she's flipping nuts," Justin muttered. "I told you to block her."

"You're not responsible for her actions," Trina said, agreeing with Justin. "I really need to get Ben home. He's been through a lot."

"We'll come with you." Joel nodded at how Ben was talking to Royal, telling the dog how much he loved him. "Royal will help Ben get over his ordeal. We'll ask Justin to make breakfast."

"That's not necessary," she began, but a police officer interrupted.

"Mr. Sullivan?" Both Justin and Joel turned toward the officer with stripes on his sleeve identifying him as Sergeant Howell. "We'd like to take your statement. Yours too," the cop added to Justin.

"I'm Joel; this is Justin. We're happy to provide statements."

Trina stepped back and subtly reached for Ben. She suspected the brothers would be tied up for a while, and she wasn't going to hold Joel to his offer of spending more time with her and Ben. "Are you hungry?" She pulled the handheld video game from her back hip pocket. "Look what I have."

"My game!" Distracted, Ben grabbed it with both hands. She led him up the path to the opening between the trees that would lead to her backyard. His face fell. "I'm sorry. I shouldn't have crawled out the window to get my game all by myself."

"No, Ben, you shouldn't have." She rested her hand on his shoulder. "You need to listen to me, Ben. We would have gotten your game for you when it was safe."

"I know." He lifted his somber gaze to meet hers. "I didn't think she would try to hurt me."

"I understand." She shivered, despite the warmth of the sun. If anything bad had happened to Ben, she wouldn't have forgiven herself.

Thanks to Joel, her son was safe. And deep down, she understood the best gift she could give Joel was to let him move on with his life.

JOEL HAD WANTED to head back to Trina's house right away but understood providing his statement about how things had gone down was important. Simmons avoided his gaze, as if feeling guilty over the way Joel had been grazed by a bullet.

He'd barely noticed at the time, as he'd been too busy hitting the ground the split-second he realized Lisa intended to fire. He'd deliberately rolled into her, knocking her off balance. Thankfully, Justin and Simmons rushed forward to disarm her, preventing her from firing again. The wound throbbed a bit now, but it could have been much worse.

"I'm sorry," Simmons muttered. "I should have taken the lead back there."

He arched a brow. "I'm the one who used my K9 to track them. It's not something you could have done for me."

"Tell me what happened, but start from the beginning," Howell said.

Joel glanced at Justin. "We met Lisa several weeks ago when she was hiking the trails in the Bighorns. She got herself good and lost, so Justin and I headed out with our K9s to find her. Royal tracked her down after a couple of hours."

"She became overly attached to Joel from the start," Justin said. "She's pretty, at least on the outside, but apparently isn't accustomed to men not falling all over themselves to date her."

"I wasn't mean or nasty, but she once told me that she could have any man she wanted." Joel grimaced at the memory. "I told her that didn't include me and that she should find someone else."

Howell frowned. "You're saying she did all of this"—he waved his arm at their surroundings—"because you wouldn't date her?"

"I know it sounds crazy." Joel hunched his shoulders, hardly able to believe it himself. "It honestly never crossed my mind that she might be responsible."

"Unbelievable," Simmons said. "A woman who looks like that could have any man she wanted."

Joel shook his head, remembering right from the start how he'd thought Lisa was too much like Bethany. Used to getting whatever she wanted. "That's the point. She couldn't have me. You need to ask her if she had help with the bomb she placed under my SUV at the rental cabin." He glanced at his K9. "Royal alerted on her scent, so I know she was there. But Royal did not alert anywhere around the cabin itself. So she either hid in the woods for hours, or she had help from some other guy."

"I can do that. We have her on attempted murder and kidnapping a minor for starters. I'd love to add arson to the list."

"She set fire to Trina's home," Justin said. "Unless she had help with that too."

Howell blew out a breath. "Okay, I'll need to reinterview Trina Warren again."

"Give her some time." Joel frowned. "She's had a rough morning."

"Sounds like you've all had a difficult morning," Simmons said.

"Let's get back to Trina's." Justin slapped Joel on the back. "You need to get that arm bandaged up."

He nodded and moved past the officers. In a low voice, he asked, "Was it my imagination, or did you notice how Trina seemed to distance herself from me?"

His twin sighed. "She cares about you, bro. The same way you care about her. Try not to mess this up."

Joel worried the warning was too late. That he'd already messed it up. Knowing that every moment Trina was in danger, barely escaping one incident after another, was his fault might be too much for her. Not that he'd led Lisa on in any way. At least, he didn't think so.

Maybe he'd flirted a bit when he and Royal had first rescued her. After all, he was single, and she was stunning, even with dirt and grime from being out in the elements all night. But that was all he'd done. He'd never kissed her or anything close to giving her the impression that he wanted to date her.

"I don't know, maybe we should head back to the ranch." Joel didn't want to pile on to Trina's already emotional day.

"Don't be a fool." Justin's tone was sharp. "I know a lovesick guy when I see one. You care about her and that little boy. Don't assume you know how she feels."

He supposed his brother had a point. At the very least, Trina deserved the truth. What she chose to do with that information was up to her.

"Come, Royal." He picked up his pace, with Royal trotting along at his side.

Justin and Stone followed more slowly. When he reached Trina's house, he hesitated, then knocked at the damaged front door. He eyed the frame, thinking it wouldn't take that long for him and Justin to replace the door and the surrounding frame. A quick trip to the hardware store and they could have it repaired by lunchtime.

Upon opening the door, Trina looked surprised to see him. "Joel, I thought you and Justin would have headed home by now."

He managed a grin. "Any chance I could borrow a few bandages? And maybe some coffee?"

"Of course." Royal snaked past her as if he owned the place. Hearing Ben's whoop of joy in greeting Royal gave him hope. At least Ben was on his side.

Or more accurately, Ben was on Royal's side.

"Sit down." Trina gestured to the kitchen chair. "I'll get the bandages. You're lucky I stocked up after Ben wiped out on his bike a few weeks ago."

He sat, looking longingly at the coffee pot. Trina must have noticed because after dumping the box of first aid supplies on the table, she filled a mug and handed it to him.

"I hope you're not left-handed." She dampened a washcloth and began to clean the wound.

"Nope." He sipped his coffee, watching her expression. She didn't flinch at the sight of blood, which was a good thing considering she was raising an eight-year-old boy.

"I already fed Ben. He was starving." She glanced at him briefly before turning her attention back to his wound. "I'd be happy to make more eggs for you and Justin."

"Are you sure?" He felt as if he were walking on a swaying bridge that might collapse under his weight at any moment. "I don't want to put you out."

"It's the least I can do." She dried his arm and applied a wide bandage over the gash. "There. All set."

"Thanks." He didn't want her to feed him out of

gratitude. He glanced over when Justin and Stone came in.

"Hey, Ben, how about we take the dogs outside for a bit?" His brother didn't hide the fact that he was giving Trina and Joel some alone time.

"Okay." Ben tossed his handheld video game aside, the one that had nearly cost the boy his life, and jumped off the sofa. "Come, Royal."

Royal seemed to understand it was playtime. His K9 followed Stone, Justin, and Ben outside.

Joel rose to his feet and caught Trina's hand. "Will you sit down for a minute?"

"Ah, sure." She looked flustered, her cheeks going pink. She dropped into the closest kitchen chair. "I—do the police need to talk to me?"

"Yes, but not now. Later." Still holding her hand, he sat beside her. "Trina, I want to apologize for everything you've been through. I swear if I had any idea Lisa could do something like this, I'd have told you."

"I don't blame you." She dropped her gaze to their clasped hands, then shook her head. "I was surprised too. She always seemed nice. A little standoffish maybe, but nice."

"I never led her on or indicated I liked her more than a casual acquaintance." Joel hesitated, feeling as if he was handling this wrong. Words were Trina's strength, not his. "If you want the truth, I purposefully avoided her."

That caused her to look up in surprise. "Why?"

"She struck me as the kind of woman who used her looks to get what she wants." He sighed. "I dated a girl like that in high school and decided never to go out with anyone like that again."

"Bethany was like that?"

He was caught off guard that Trina knew Bethany's name. "Yeah. Big time. Although it took me a while to figure it out. I was young and stupid, letting my hormones override my brain. I was so much happier without her."

"I had no idea." Her brown eyes were wide. "I thought you and Bethany were perfect together."

"Not even close." He tightened his grip on her hand. "I'll be honest, Trina. I avoided relationships for a long time. Had no intention of settling down like so many of my siblings have. But spending these past few days with you has made me realize that you are everything I've always wanted in a woman."

"Me?" She gaped at him. "That's impossible. I'm nothing like you!"

He tipped his head to the side. "Are you sure about that? You're brave, fiercely protective of your family, and easygoing."

"But, Joel, I could never camp in a tent overnight in the woods. Or do any of the search and rescue stuff you and your siblings do. I'm a homebody." She tugged her hand from his. "I appreciate your kindness, but I don't see how this can work out."

"I never asked you to go camping." He didn't hide his exasperation. "Or to go on any SAR missions. I don't care if you're not the outdoorsy type. I think you're amazing. Not just your ability to write books, something I could never in a million years do, but the way you put your entire life on hold for Ben? That alone tells me everything I need to know about your character."

When she still looked at him skeptically, he tried again.

"You're pretty, smart, unselfish, and is it okay if I kiss you now?"

Now her cheeks went bright red. "Joel, really, you don't have to . . ."

He threw up his hands in a gesture of frustration. "I love you, Trina. I wasn't interested in settling down one bit until I met you and Ben. And if you don't feel the same way, that's fine. I'll walk away right now." He held her gaze. "But I need you to say the words. To tell me you don't feel the same way."

She stared at him for a long moment, then rose and stepped closer. "I can't, Joel, because I do feel the same way."

"Really?" It was his turn to be taken by surprise.

"I've fallen in love with you too." She smiled up at him, rose up on her tippy toes, and kissed him.

This was where Trina belonged, in the circle of his arms. He pulled her close and deepened their kiss, trying to tell her without words how much he loved her.

"Hey, bro, whoops." Joel wanted to kick his twin for his lousy timing. "Ah, sorry, but Griff is here and wants to talk."

Rotten timing. Joel ended their kiss but didn't even look toward his brother. "Later."

"Now." Justin flashed an unrepentant grin. "He wants to talk to Trina too."

"Me? Why?" Trina took a step back, breaking off their embrace. He reluctantly let her go but was re-assured by the way she'd kissed him.

"I guess he found your sister's ex, and the guy actually admitted to being there when she crashed her bike into the tree." Justin gestured behind him. "He'll give you the details."

Trina blanched. Joel took her hand, and said, "I'm here for you."

"I know." She squeezed his fingers. "Let's do this."

His FBI brother-in-law-to-be was outside talking to the local police about the events surrounding Lisa Schilling and her kidnapping Ben. When Griff saw him and Trina, he excused himself and crossed over. Eyeing the bandage on Joel's arm, Griff shook his head. "Good thing it's not serious."

"Just a scratch." Joel placed his right arm around Trina. Ben was still in the yard playing with the dogs. "What's up with Peter Thomas being with Trina's sister when she died?"

"I grilled Peter for hours late last night when I finally tracked him down at his favorite bar." Griff looked slightly annoyed that the Laramie cops hadn't found him first. "I finally got him to admit he and Evie had gone biking together. They also had a rip-roaring fight again over the money he owed her, one that had Evie storming off in anger." Griff's gaze was apologetic. "It sounds to me like Peter took off after your sister, which only made her go faster down that hill. That's when she lost control of her bike and crashed into the tree."

Trina gripped him hard. "Are we sure he didn't push her or mess with her bike?"

Griff hesitated, then shrugged. "I don't think so. To be honest, I believed his story. Peter appeared relieved to have the truth out in the open. I think his role in the crash has been haunting him."

"Any chance you can find the bike to make sure?" Joel asked.

"The police had what was left of the bike inspected, and as far as they could tell, the brakes weren't tampered with." Griff looked at Trina. "Are you okay?"

"Better now." She smiled and hugged Joel. "Much better now."

Griff looked from Joel to Trina and back again. Then he grinned. "Glad to hear it."

Joel knew his feelings were plain to see. He continued to hold Trina close, and Griff turned back to the cops.

"I love you so much," he whispered.

"I love you too." She rested her head in the hollow of his shoulder. "I'm not sure what I did to deserve someone like you."

"That's my line." He watched Ben with Royal and Stone, realizing he'd been wrong all this time.

He absolutely wanted a family of his own. And without his even realizing it, God had answered his prayers.

EPILOGUE

Three weeks later . . .

Trina couldn't believe how much Ben loved being at the ranch. As much as he liked school and had made new friends, he still preferred spending weekends at the ranch.

"Can we go to the ranch again?" Ben's expression was hopeful as he ate his after-school snack of peanut butter crackers.

"Yes, Joel invited us to stay this weekend." Sometimes their time together was cut short with search and rescue missions, but she understood. As someone who'd depended on Joel's and Royal's expertise, she would never stand in their way of helping others.

And now that she'd finished her book, she had

ideas of incorporating Joel's work into her next mystery.

The house next door was up for sale. Lisa was still behind bars, having been implicated in the SUV explosion by Gerry Suchan, who'd turned on her in a heartbeat. He'd claimed Lisa offered him three grand to do the job, half up front. She had never paid the second half of the money. Gerry had claimed he hadn't done any of the other things, and his alibi had proven that. Still, he'd go to jail, too, for the role he'd played in the bombing-for-hire scheme. Burt Jones had found Lisa on one of the gas station videos filling up a portable can with fuel an hour before Trina's house was set on fire. With that, the Cody PD had added arson to the list of charges against her.

A knock at the door had her spinning toward it. With a frown, she walked over to answer it. When she saw Joel standing there, she was surprised. "Hey, what are you doing here?"

"I couldn't wait." He opened the door that he and his brother had replaced and gave Royal room to come inside. "I have a surprise."

"You do?" She should have known, he looked like a kid holding a candy bar behind his back. "What's that?" She really hoped he didn't want her to go camping.

"Hi, Joel! Hi, Royal!" Ben slid off his chair to greet the dog.

Joel winked, opened the door, and bent to pick up a small black puppy. Her eyes rounded in surprise, then grew damp with tears. "You didn't!"

"I did." He looked alarmed. "You're not upset?"

"Not at all." She was touched by his thoughtfulness. "A promise is a promise."

"Ben, I'd like you to meet King." He set the young lab down on the floor.

"A puppy? For me?" Ben's eyes widened. "Really?"

"Yep. I named him King because we named our dogs after national parks, like King's Canyon. But if you want to change it, we can." Joel grinned as the puppy ran toward Ben and tried to crawl into his lap. "That's up to you."

"Hi, King. Hi, boy." Ben gathered the pup close. "I love King."

"Good." He reached for Trina, giving her a quick hug and a kiss. "Another family backed out of taking him at the last minute, so I pounced on the opportunity. And don't worry, I'll help you and Ben train him."

"You'd better." She sighed, thinking of the sleepless nights ahead. "We're going to need help."

"Trina." He held her gaze. "I was going to wait until this weekend when we were with the family, but they can be overwhelming and nosy, so I'm going to ask you now." He pulled a small box from his pocket, opened it, and held out the ring. "Will you marry me?"

"Yeah, will you?" Ben echoed. She glanced at him in surprise. Her son grinned. "Joel asked me if it was okay to marry you, and I said yes."

Now the tears spilled over. "Yes, Joel! Yes! I would be honored to marry you."

He kissed her again, then pulled out the ring and slid it onto her finger. "If you don't like this, we'll get something else."

"I love it." She couldn't have cared less about the ring, but the one he'd chosen was a simple, sparkling diamond. "It's perfect." She stepped into his arms and kissed him again. "There is one condition."

"Oh yeah?" He looked worried, which was cute. "What's that?"

"Please, Joel, no camping." When he blinked, she added, "I mean like ever."

He threw back his head and laughed. "Ah, Trina. I'll never make you do anything you don't want to."

"Good. That's good." She breathed a sigh of relief. They still needed to decide living arrangements, but she wasn't concerned. Her job was flexible. And Ben loved the ranch.

"Uh-oh, I think King has to get busy!" Ben

jumped up, still clutching the puppy, and ran toward the door. Joel opened it for him, then grinned at her.

"See? The pup is practically housebroken already."

"Yeah, right." She laughed and slipped her arm around his waist. Ben put King down on the grass, urging him to get busy while the puppy squatted to do his thing.

In that moment, she saw their future together as a family. Gazing up at the blue sky, she silently thanked God for the gift of Joel's love.

I HOPE you enjoyed Joel and Trina's story! Are you ready to read about Justin and Raine in *Scent of Evil*? Click Here!

DEAR READER

Thanks for reading *Scent of Fury*! I hope you enjoyed Joel and Trina's story. I'm having so much fun writing about the Sullivan family. I hope you are loving them as much as I am. And please stay tuned for *Scent of Evil*, which will be Justin and Raine's story. You won't want to miss that one.

Don't forget, you can purchase ebooks or audiobooks directly from my website and will receive a 15% discount by using the code **LauraScott15.**

I adore hearing from my readers! I can be found through my website at https://www.laurascottbook s.com, via Facebook at https://www.facebook.com/ LauraScottBooks, Instagram at https://www.insta gram.com/laurascottbooks/, and Twitter https://twit ter.com/laurascottbooks. Please take a moment to subscribe to my YouTube channel at youtube.-

com/@LauraScottBooks-wr1xl?sub_confirmation=1. Also take a moment to sign up for my monthly newsletter to learn about my new book releases! All subscribers receive a free novella not available for purchase on any platform.

Until next time,

Laura Scott

PS. Keep reading for a sneak peek of *Scent of Evil* . . .

SCENT OF EVIL

Chapter One

US Marshal Raine Whitman stared down at the dead man lying at the side of the road. The victim had been shot in the head at close range just outside of Casper, Wyoming. A mixture of anger and fear hummed through her blood stream. There was no doubt in her mind this was the work of her escaped prisoner, Allen Decker. The man was a sexual predator who'd finally gotten caught back when he'd abducted Raine's niece, Ginny Clark. After Ginny had managed to escape, her description of Decker had helped the local sheriff's deputy find and arrest him.

Now, two years after his conviction, Decker had

escaped with the help of his creepy underground pedophile network. The details were foggy, and she knew her boss Mike Rowe was still piecing his escape plan together. One thing they knew for sure was that the prison van transporting Decker to the hospital had been badly damaged in a T-bone crash. The van driver had been killed and so had the pedophile in the second car.

Yet Decker was missing.

How the crash had been prearranged, they still weren't sure. Raine was convinced Decker had some help from the inside, maybe even his lawyer who could have passed messages back and forth on Decker's behalf. Either way, that was a moot point. The problem now was that Decker was out of prison and on the move. And despite the fact that his escape had taken place on Interstate 80 about fifteen miles from the prison, the moment this call had come in, Raine had suspected Decker was responsible.

Raine and her other US Marshal colleagues needed to find him before he could kill another innocent bystander or abduct any young girls. Like Ginny.

Keeping her expression impassive, she turned to the Wyoming State Trooper. "Do you have an ID on this guy yet?"

"Nope. His wallet was stolen, and as you can see by what's left of his face, we don't have enough to run him through the facial recognition database. As soon as the crime scene techs get here, we can run his fingerprints. Hopefully, he's in the system. If not?" The trooper shrugged. "We may be out of luck."

She swallowed a curse, a bad habit she'd given up when Ginny had spent time with her this past summer. "We need an ID to figure out what vehicle Decker is driving."

"I know." Trooper Wade Callum gestured to the highway. "We came to Casper from the south. If your convict is responsible for this murder, he could go either way from here. Either heading west toward the Wind River Reservation or north toward Buffalo and the Bighorn Mountains. If you ask me, he's more likely to go west to the reservation. He may find it easier to hide on the reservation than in other cities or towns."

Raine swallowed hard, trying not to show her panic. She didn't for one minute think Decker was heading east. She had a very bad feeling he was going north toward Buffalo, where her niece lived. Her boss didn't agree, claiming Decker was too smart to do something so obvious.

Was she wrong? Had this man been shot and

killed by someone other than Decker? No, she didn't believe in coincidences. This had to be Decker's work. "Any idea how long ago this guy has been murdered? Decker escaped three hours ago." Three hours. Three long, frustrating hours.

Trooper Callum scratched his chin. "I'm no expert, but based on the flies and buzzards overhead who've already made a meal of this guy's face and hands, I'd say at least an hour or two."

"Thanks." Raine reached for her phone just as it rang. Seeing FBI Griff Flannery's name on the screen, she quickly answered. "Thanks for calling me back. I need SAR help in tracking an escaped prisoner, Allen Decker. He's a convicted pedophile who has already killed two men since his escape and should be considered armed and dangerous. Not to mention a threat to young girls everywhere."

"I heard about his escape." Griff's tone was somber. "I have asked for help from the Sullivan K9 Search and Rescue Ranch. My brother-in-law Justin Sullivan and his K9, Stone, are ready to go, but they're in Greybull at the moment."

"Great. Please ask Justin to head toward Buffalo, I'll meet him there." She had heard all about the Sullivan K9 teams and how great they were at finding missing people. "We may need more than one team searching for him, though."

"That's fine," Griff said. "Trevor Sullivan and his K9, Archie, can head out, too, if needed. I'm currently in Cheyenne for a meeting with the governor, but I know that all law enforcement agencies in the area are on the lookout for this guy."

That isn't good enough, she thought wearily. But she refrained from stating the obvious. "What about getting a couple of police choppers in the air?"

"We can deploy choppers, but that works better if we have a description of the vehicle." Griff sounded apologetic. "We can't just burn fuel by flying around without knowing who we're looking for. Especially as bow-hunting season is in full swing. The traffic on the interstate and local highways is higher than normal this time of the year."

She bit back her anger. Griff was right. Just sending choppers into the air without a target to focus on would be a waste of money. And it could even backfire. If Decker saw the choppers, he may find another vehicle to steal, killing the occupants the way he had this poor man lying in the ditch. "I'm hoping we'll have an ID on our most recent victim soon and that it will provide a vehicle description. I also think Decker is heading to Buffalo, where my sister and her daughter lives. I need you to get the local authorities to check on them."

"Consider it done. I plan to head back to the

ranch in an hour or so." She heard muffled voices in the background, as if the meeting Griff mentioned was breaking up. "My brother-in-law Logan Fletcher is a pilot; he's chartering a hunting party into the Bighorns and said he'd keep an eye out for Decker."

That was encouraging. They had Allen Decker's face plastered on every news station across the country. Someone somewhere would hopefully see him and report the sighting to the authorities. "Thanks."

"I gave Justin your cell number," Griff said. "That way you can communicate with him directly."

"That's fine." Raine preferred it that way. She strode toward her SUV. "Have him call me right away."

"Understood," Griff agreed. "Keep in touch, Raine. If you get more clues as to where this guy is, let me know and we'll deploy more resources to find him."

"Will do. Thanks." She ended the call as she slid in behind the wheel of her SUV. She quickly started the car and hit the road, heading north on Highway 25.

Stomping her foot hard on the accelerator, she pushed the engine as much as she could. Speed limits didn't matter to her, but she soon found Griff was right about the traffic. As a US Marshal, she didn't have a light bar on her vehicle, but she flashed her lights to encourage drivers to move out of the way. She called her niece, Ginny, but the eleven-year-old didn't answer. She tried her sister, Cami, too, with the same results. The cell coverage in Buffalo could be spotty, especially since her sister worked at the Wild Buffalo Hotel, which was outside of town. She left both her sister and niece a message to be careful and to call her back as soon as they could.

Maybe she was wrong about Decker going to find her niece. If he was smart, he'd find one of his creepy buddies and stay off the radar until the heat of the search died down. But having looked into Decker's soulless eyes during the trial, she knew he was sick and evil. And capable of anything.

She made good time for the next thirty-five minutes and hoped to be in Buffalo sooner than she'd originally anticipated.

Her phone rang, a strange number flashing on the screen. Remembering Griff saying he was giving her number to Justin, she quickly answered. "Whitman."

"Marshal Whitman? This is Justin Sullivan. I understand you need help."

"Yes." That was one way of putting it. "Call me Raine. How quickly can you get to Buffalo, Wyoming?"

"I happened to be in Greybull when Griff called, so I'm heading that way now. I can be there in thirty minutes, maybe a little longer as I'm pulling two horses in a trailer, which will slow me down."

"Okay, we should get there about the same time, then." Raine was glad she wouldn't have to wait too long. "I'm giving you my sister Camille's address. She's working, but on a Saturday, my niece should be around. I called but had to leave a message. I want you to get there as soon as possible."

"Got it," Justin said when she'd provided the information. "Did you notify the police too?"

"Yes, Griff was going to send a request to the local sheriff's department to head over there." Knowing police and Justin were on their way helped her feel better. It bothered her that Ginny hadn't answered her call, then she belatedly remembered Cami telling her Ginny had a part-time job working at a local horse farm, mucking stalls and other chores. "If Ginny isn't at my sister's, she could be at the Lucky Charm horse farm."

"Okay, why don't you call them?" Justin suggested. "That way they can keep an eye on her too."

"I will." She hesitated, then added, "I hope I'm not dragging you out to Buffalo for no good reason. My boss doesn't think my hunch is correct."

"Don't worry about it." Justin didn't sound upset

or annoyed with the possibility. "I'd rather be safe than sorry."

"Me too. Thanks." She ended the call and quickly asked her phone to call the Lucky Charm. Unfortunately, her call went straight to voice mail.

Why wasn't anyone answering their phone?

Raine left a message, then focused her attention on driving. She'd lost some time while making her calls and hit the gas to make up for it. A few minutes later, Nancy Drago, co-owner of the Lucky Charm, returned her call. "Raine? I just listened to your message. Ginny isn't working here this weekend; she has a project due for school."

"Okay, thanks." Raine hesitated, then decided against going into the whole story. "If you see Ginny, please have her call me right away."

"Okay." Nancy ended the call.

If Ginny wasn't working, then why hadn't she answered her phone? The thought nagged at her for the next several miles.

She was ten miles outside of Buffalo when her phone rang again. Seeing Ginny's name on the screen had her quickly punching the button to answer. "Hey, Ginny. Thanks for returning my call."

"Auntie Raine? He's here." Ginny's voice was barely a whisper. "I'm hiding, but he's outside, trying to get in."

An icy wave of terror washed over her. "Who, Decker? Are you sure?"

"Yes!" There was no mistaking the panic in Ginny's hushed voice. "What if he finds me?"

"I'm on my way and so are the police." Raine wasn't sure why the sheriff's deputies weren't there already. "Did you call 911?"

"Yes, but please hurry." Ginny sounded desperate. Then Raine heard a crashing sound in the background. Had Decker kicked in a door or a window?

"Ginny? Can you hear me? Stay on the line . . ." but it was too late.

The other end of the call had gone dead.

JUSTIN SULLIVAN MADE good time along the back roads to Buffalo despite hauling the horse trailer. He had taken the pair of geldings to be seen by a blacksmith for new shoes. As the third youngest of nine siblings, he had often sought solace in the barn with the horses when he was young, and he was their primary caretaker now.

He could do just about anything with the animals, except replace their shoes.

Justin eyed his yellow lab, Stone, stretched out in the back crate area of his specially designed SUV. His K9 was a great tracker, yet he couldn't deny feeling a bit of apprehension related to his upcoming mission. He'd done hundreds of search and rescue missions over the six years he and his family had been running the ranch, but never for an escaped convict.

Not just any convict. A sexual predator with a habit of attacking young girls. The thought of this man getting his hands on another young victim made him sick.

He pushed the speed limit as much as he dared, considering his cargo. He would have rather run the horses back to the ranch, but there wasn't time. One of the problems of doing SAR missions in Wyoming was not only the mountainous terrain, but also the miles of distance between towns.

Having brought up Allen Decker's mug shot on his phone, Justin made a point of eyeballing the drivers of the vehicles around him. None looked like Decker, although he knew it was possible the guy was using some sort of disguise.

When his phone rang, displaying US Marshal Raine Whitman's name on the screen, he answered. In the back crate, Stone lifted his head, his ears pricked forward with interest. "Raine?"

"Decker has Ginny." Her voice held a note of panic. "He's in Buffalo and has my niece."

The statement shocked him. "Are you sure?"

"She called, said he was there. She was hiding,

but I heard him breaking in." Her voice trembled, then steadied. "The police should be there by now too. Maybe they'll be able to stop him. How close are you?"

"Five miles." Justin instinctively pressed harder on the gas.

"Hurry. I may be a few minutes behind you." Raine abruptly ended the call.

Justin couldn't believe Decker had gone after Raine's niece in Buffalo. Why would he do such a thing? The perp had to know that Raine would anticipate his movements.

As the highway curved, he slowed, double-checking the trailer in the rearview mirror. He used his GPS system to reach Raine's sister's home, nestled toward the back of a dead-end road. He pulled over to the side and hit the release for the back hatch. After the long drive, Stone didn't hesitate to jump down.

"Come, Stone." He ran toward the police cruiser, his lab keeping pace beside him. There was the high-pitched sound of a small engine, maybe a four-wheeler or a motorbike. He frowned when he saw a rusty black Ford F150 truck. The way it was parked down the street made him think Decker had driven it there. He caught up to the sheriff's deputy, someone he didn't recognize. His name tag identified him as Bolton. "Did you find Ginny?"

"Who are you?" Deputy Bolton frowned, then he must have noticed Stone. "Oh, you're one of the Sullivans I've heard so much about."

"Justin." He nodded and gestured to his K9. "This is Stone. We're here because there's a pedophile on the loose, and Ginny is in danger."

He'd barely finished talking when an SUV zoomed up the street, stopping so abruptly the vehicle jerked. A second later, a lean woman with long dark hair strode toward them. From the tense expression on her face, he knew she was Raine Whitman. She was dressed in jeans and a long-sleeved shirt with a marshal badge on her chest. Raine glanced from him to the deputy. "Where's Ginny?"

Deputy Bolton threw up his hands. "I don't know who Ginny is, but there's nobody here."

Raine paled, then bolted past the deputy heading for the house. Instinctively, Justin followed with Stone beside him. When he noticed how the front door was damaged, he feared the worst.

Allen Decker had been there.

"Ginny!" Raine shouted as she moved through the house. Stone sniffed with interest as they followed. His stomach twisted more when he saw the back door was open. Raine ran outside, glancing frantically from side to side. "Ginny!"

Justin paused, scanning the interior. Aside of

the broken front door, there was no sign of a struggle. Then again, Raine had said the guy was armed.

A young girl couldn't resist against a man with a gun.

Raine whirled toward him. "Can you track him?"

"Stone can." He gestured to his lab. "Do you want Stone to track your niece or the perp?"

"Both." She dragged her hands through her hair, her expression grim. "They couldn't have gotten too far on foot."

"Are you sure they're not using something else? When I got here, I thought I heard a small engine in the distance."

Raine's blue eyes widened in horror, and she spun around to head back outside. There was a shed off to the side, the door hanging ajar. It only took her a moment to look inside and glance back at him. "The four-wheeler is gone."

Not good. Justin jerked his thumb toward the road. "I hope you can ride because our best chance at finding Ginny is to use my horses."

"Horses!" Raine looked relieved. "I can ride."

"Good. I'll get them out of the trailer and geared up." He was glad he'd included saddles and bridles for the trip. He'd intended to ride Blaze in the area where the piece of his parents' crashed plane had been found until Griff's call had come through. "You need to get Stone a scent source for your niece. Dirty socks or a shirt would work."

"Okay." To her credit, Raine didn't waste time arguing.

"Come, Stone." Justin jogged around the house to his horse trailer. He opened the back and quickly led Timber and Blaze from the trailer. The horses stomped their feet and tossed their heads as if glad to be out of the trailer.

Justin had just finished saddling and bridling them when Raine returned holding two bags of clothing. Seeing the faded orange fabric in one bag, he realized that one held Decker's scent. The other bag was smaller and contained a green T-shirt and pair of dirty socks inside.

"We need to hurry," Raine said. "I don't know how much of a head start he has."

Considering Decker was on a four-wheeler, Justin understood her concern. Especially since he knew what this creep was capable of. "Here, hold the reins for Timber. You'll take him; I'll ride Blaze. Before we saddle up, though, I need to gather some items for Stone."

A look of impatience flashed in her eyes. Ignoring it, he turned to his SUV. His backpack was ready to go, but he took a moment to check the contents, then rummaged for extra items, specifically water bottles. He tucked several into Blaze's saddlebag. Lastly, he removed his sidearm from the pack and quickly slipped his belt through the holster and snaking the belt back through his jeans. He tucked the weapon inside.

Then he took the two plastic bags from Raine's hand. He used Decker's first, offering it to Stone. "Decker," he said. "This is Decker."

Stone sniffed for a long moment, then looked up at him, tail wagging. The grim situation wasn't completely lost on Stone. The dog's ears were perked forward. His K9 was all about playing the search game.

He poured some water into a collapsible bowl. Stone lowered his head, took a few laps, then looked up expectantly. Justin opened the second bag. "This is Ginny."

Again, Stone sniffed the contents of the bag. Justin used the time to pack the collapsible bowl away, then rose to his feet. He threw out his hand. "Search! Search Decker and Ginny!"

Stone lowered his nose to the ground and trotted toward the black Ford truck. Justin decided to let the dog alert there, as it would help ramp up Stone's excitement for the search to come.

Justin had subtly pulled the stuffed penguin from his pack, anticipating Stone's alert. The dog sniffed along the bottom of the driver's side door, sat, and let out a sharp bark.

"Good boy!" He tossed the penguin for Stone who leaped up to catch it. "Good boy, Stone. You found Decker."

Stone frolicked with the toy for a moment, then trotted back to him. After regurgitating the toy into his hand, the dog waited. "Search! Search Decker and Ginny!"

This time, Stone turned and sniffed along the path to the house. Justin hurried over to where Raine stood next to Timber. "Do you need a leg up?"

"Please." She reached up to grasp the saddle horn. He laced his palms together so she could step into them, then hoisted her up onto Timber's back. He quickly adjusted the stirrups, then swung up onto Blaze.

"Stay close," he advised.

"Don't worry, I will." Raine looked determined to keep up, no matter what.

Stone was all the way up to the house now, sniffing along the front porch. Stone sat and let out another sharp bark.

"Good boy, Stone." Justin didn't reward the dog this time. The job was far from done. "Search! Search Decker and Ginny!"

His K9 lifted his nose to the air. Justin took note of the breeze coming from the east and hoped Decker wasn't smart enough to stay downhill from the wind. Stone trotted around the side of the house. Giving Blaze a gentle nudge with his heels, he urged the gelding to follow.

"Wait, what are we supposed to do?" Deputy Bolton asked.

"First call FBI Agent Griff Flannery, let him know where we are and that we're following Decker. Then get more cops into the woods," Justin suggested. "We're going to need backup."

"Also, please call my sister, Camille Clark," Raine added. "She works at the Wild Buffalo Hotel. She needs to know Ginny is missing."

Justin kept his gaze on Stone. His K9 trotted at a quick pace, one he could easily keep up with on Blaze. He made a note of the time, knowing he'd have to give Stone frequent rest breaks.

Maybe even carrying the dog on his saddle for a while if needed.

He and Raine didn't talk much as he followed Stone into the wooded terrain. He caught the occasional glimpse of tire tracks in the earth. Stone was hot on the trail, which was good. But the hour was already going on two in the afternoon, and he didn't want to imagine what would happen if they didn't find Ginny before dark.

Glancing back over his shoulder, he was glad to see Raine was keeping up. Timber was a calm and steady equine.

He ducked beneath a low-hanging branch as

Blaze got too close. Then his mount gathered himself to climb a steep incline. Stone was still leading the way, and he kept his eye on his K9's yellow coat.

When they reached the top of the ridge, he pulled up on the reins, searching the ground for tire tracks. They veered off to the right, and that's where Stone was headed too. He turned Blaze in that direction when the sharp echo of a gunshot rang out. He instinctively ducked as a bullet whizzed past.

Decker was shooting at them!